Snowbound
WITH THE
BARONET

Snowbound
WITH THE
BARONET

DEBORAH HALE

To Wally and Irma, who seized their second chance at love.

Chapter One

Wiltshire, England ~ January 1814

"**Y**OU DON'T NEED to do this, Cassie." Lady Viola Whitney clasped her sister's hand as if she intended to prevent her going by physical force.

That would have been impossible, of course. At five-and-twenty, Viola was the elder by more than a year, but Cassandra had long ago surpassed her in height and strength of will.

"Please reconsider." Viola eased her grip in favor of a heartfelt appeal, which had a far better chance of succeeding. "How will we manage without you?"

"Admirably, I'm certain." Cassandra strove to ignore the pang her sister's words provoked. "It is high time you all had an opportunity to make decisions without me to always take the lead. If that proves too difficult, you can consult Letty or Lord Highworth."

Bundled up against the cold of early January, the Whitney sisters stood outside the village inn. A little way off, their two younger sisters, their stepmother and her friend Mrs. Davis were watching for the arrival of the stagecoach.

"Don't be flippant," Viola snapped in an uncharacteristic flash of temper. "Have you given any thought to what your absence will mean for us? How am I to bear the full responsibility for Miranda and Evie on my own, to say nothing of how lonesome I shall be without you? I shall be distracted with worry about you, dancing attendance on that vexatious old gorgon. I fear she will drive you mad within a fortnight!"

"How melodramatic! That isn't like you, Vi." Cassandra forced a laugh and that she hoped would reassure her sister. "I admit Aunt Augusta can be rather … *querulous* at times but she only bullies people who let her. I refuse to put up with any such nonsense. As for my thinking about the rest of you, my motives are not entirely selfish. You know Aunt Augusta has promised that if I come to live as her companion she will give Evie a Season in London. The rest of us had our chance. It is only fair that she does too, poor dear."

Cassandra cast an affectionate glance toward their youngest sister who retained enough of a girlish appearance that she should not attract too much unfavorable attention making her debut at the advanced age of nineteen. She would miss Evie's high spirits, Miranda's artistic fancies and Letty's motherly gentleness. Most of all she would miss Viola's sweet temper and good sense. But she must not think of that or she might start to blubber. Then Vi would never let her go.

"Don't forget," she added as much to remind herself as her sister, "there is Mrs. Davis to think of, as well. Housekeeper to a viscountess will be an excellent situation for her."

That was the other part of the bargain Cassandra had struck with their great-aunt in an exchange of letters that autumn. Now that her plans were all coming to fruition at last, Cassandra found herself torn between anticipation and dread. Those made her shiver quite as much as the gust of damp, icy wind that swirled her cloak and tugged at her skirts.

"The stage coach!" Evie squealed. "I see it coming."

Viola's fair complexion grew paler in contrast to the frost-nipped apples of her cheeks. Though she lowered her voice, it took on a tone of increasing desperation. "A woman capable as Mrs. Davis could surely find another position if you were to change your mind. And Evie is not pining for a Season. Ours brought no great joy to the rest of us, in case you have forgotten."

"Forgotten?" Cassandra drew herself up. "No indeed. I remember all too well, but it would be different for Evie …

with Father gone."

Their late father had managed to spoil the first tender romances of his three eldest daughters. Vi might not resent him for it, but Cassandra lacked her sister's forbearance.

Viola opened her mouth to protest but Cassandra set hers in a resolute line. "There is no turning back now, dearest. I *must* do this, not just for Evie and Mrs. Davis but for myself. You know how much I dislike being beholden to anyone, even as kind a friend as Lord Highworth. With Aunt Augusta I shall feel I am earning my keep and contributing to the support of my family. Without that sense of independence, I could not go on."

"You are too proud." The beginning of a tear glittered in Viola's wide grey eyes. "I believe it is the reigning passion of your heart, even more than love. You cannot blame Father for that."

Cassandra recoiled from her sister's words. Was Vi implying that her pride was as much at fault as their father's machinations for destroying her chance of happiness with Sir Brandon Calvert?

"Indeed I *can* blame Father," she retorted. "And I do. I inherited my pride from him as surely as my dark hair and my brown eyes. Perhaps that is why we never got on — because I am too much like him while you are entirely like Mother."

She had no memories of their mother, but the miniature that was one of their most treasured possessions bore a striking likeness to Vi. How different might their lives have been if Mother had lived to bear a son?

Cassandra turned her mind from that thought. Miranda spent far too much time yearning for a past beyond recapture and a rosy future that was only a wishful dream. *She* prided herself on dealing with the world as she found it and making what she could of it. She was trying to do that now, if only Vi would let her.

"It is too late to argue," Cassandra caught her sister in a fierce embrace. "If we do not stop, I shan't have time to bid the others a proper farewell. I promise to write you long, boring letters from Noughtly Hall and we shall see each other next year when you bring Evie to London. If I feel myself going mad, I promise I shall leave at once and return home straight away."

"See that you do." Viola drew back, catching her quivering lower lip between her teeth. "And try not to make your letters too boring, or we shall never believe you wrote them."

"We have a bargain." Cassandra spun away from her elder sister, before Vi glimpsed any shadow of doubt in her eyes.

She turned toward the younger two, who seemed more excited than grieved at her going. "Don't give Vi and Letty any trouble now or I shall come straight home from Noughtly and put you both in line."

Miranda and Evelina paid no heed to their sister's brusque tone but each gave her an affectionate squeeze and vowed to be on their best behavior.

Then it was Letty's turn. "Take care of yourself my dear. It is good of you to do this for Evie and Mrs. Davis, but I would expect no less of you."

Her stepmother's admiring tone made Cassandra squirm. This undertaking was not some noble sacrifice, as Letty seemed to think, but an escape from the dependence she could no longer bear.

By now the stagecoach had arrived and Cassandra's final minutes in Charnwood were lost in a rush to secure their luggage. She and Mrs. Davis climbed inside to discover they had the whole box to themselves. As the vehicle pulled away, she waved and called to her family with an air of confident excitement that was not altogether feigned.

Only when they were out of sight did she allow her nagging misgivings to subdue her spirits.

"Oh look," chirped Mrs. Davis, pointing out the carriage window. "It is starting to snow. How pretty it will make the countryside look."

Cassandra gave an absent nod. This part of England did

not often get much snow. The winter landscape was usually a study in shades of dull brown. A soft blanket of pure white would make for a pleasant change. "I hope it will not impede our journey."

She doubted it would. Any snow that did fall on the Chalk Counties of southern England usually melted away almost as fast as it came. But December had been unusually cold and the bare ground was frozen stiff.

Two hours later the snow was falling very hard, making it impossible to see much beyond the edge of the road. The accumulation of snow Cassandra glimpsed there made her suspect it had been falling here longer than back in Charnwood. The poor coach horses must be finding it hard going for their speed was growing slower and slower. When the coach climbed a gentle rise, Cassandra wondered if she and Mrs. Davis would be obliged to get out and push. Descending the far slope proved a different problem as the rear of the coach skidded from side to side.

Mrs. Davis gave a little squeal of fright then cast Cassandra an apologetic glance. Clearly the poor woman did not want to alarm her.

"I wonder how much farther it is to Noughtly Hall?" She rubbed her gloved hand to clear a circle on the fogged window.

Cassandra gave an exaggerated shrug. "Not above twenty miles I expect, but at the rate we are going Heaven only knows when we shall reach there."

This would be a little adventure she could relate to her sisters in her first letter home. She hoped Viola and Letty would not be too worried about her on account of the snow.

Before she could think of any reassuring words to offer Mrs. Davis, Cassandra heard the coach driver bellow at the horses to stop. She feared that might not be the best idea. If the poor creatures lost what little momentum they had, who could say whether they would be able to get started again.

"It is another carriage." Mrs. Davis peered out into the whirling whiteness. "I believe it has gotten stuck in the snow."

As Cassandra leaned forward to see if she could make out anything, she heard someone having a loud exchange with the coachman. No doubt they were requesting assistance. Their carriage listed to one side, as if a wheel might have broken. The other vehicle was smaller than the stagecoach with the elegant shape of a private travelling equipage. Clearly it must belong to a family of considerable fortune. Bad roads were egalitarian — treating an earl's barouche and a farmer's pony cart all the same.

"I wonder how long those poor people have been stranded here," Mrs. Davis mused.

"I believe we are about to find out." Cassandra drew back from the window and scrambled over to sit beside her travelling companion. She had spied a snow-covered gentleman leading a heavily cloaked lady toward the stagecoach.

An instant later, the door flew open and the lady clambered inside.

"What ghastly weather!" she cried, pulling one hand from a lavish fur muff to brush away the snowflakes that clung to her cloak. "I was terrified we might be stuck here for days and freeze to death."

She cast a appraising glance over Cassandra and Mrs. Davis as she took a seat opposite them. Cassandra sensed they had been judged respectable enough to address but nothing more. She had no opportunity to take offense, for the gentleman climbed in after his companion. He had taken care to brush himself off *before* entering.

"We beg your pardon, ladies, for any inconvenience we have caused you. The arrival of you coach was providential for us."

The moment he began to speak, Cassandra fancied all the air had been sucked from the coach box. Heat flamed in her cheeks and her stomach felt as if she were tumbling down a steep hill inside a barrel. Averting her face from him, she gazed out the other window as if she could see something of urgent interest through the fogged glass.

Would Sir Brandon Calvert still consider their meeting providential, she wondered, when he discovered her identity?

Brandon sank onto the stagecoach seat with a sense of overwhelming relief. Their carriage had thrown a wheel more than an hour ago and he'd been afraid Imogene would work herself into hysterics at any moment. He had never been so happy to hear the muffled rumble of approaching hoofbeats and the rattle of harness.

He'd been prepared to pay half his fortune to coax one of the inside passengers to surrender their seat to Imogene. The coach driver assured him that would not be necessary since the vehicle carried only a pair of ladies bound for Bath. There had been outside perches for Brandon's coachman and footman as well as room in the boot for the few articles of luggage that had not been sent ahead to their destination. His horses could be unhitched and tethered to the stagecoach.

His party would take refuge at the next inn until the snow abated and someone could be sent to repair the carriage. Imogene would likely bemoan their delay in getting to Lady Norrington's house party, but that could not be helped. At least they would be warm and fed.

He apologized to the other passengers as he and Imogene settled onto the seat opposite them. A bespectacled lady of middle age greeted his words with a welcoming smile, but the other occupant turned her face away. No doubt she resented the interruption of her journey and the necessity of sharing the coach box with two more people. He could not blame her, he supposed, though he hoped he would have shown greater charity if their situations had been reversed.

"My gardener tried to warn me there was snow coming." Brandon strove to thaw the hostile chill he sensed from the lady. "I should have listened to him and postponed our journey, for he has an uncanny knack for predicting the weather."

"If we'd only set off yesterday as I wanted to," Imogene grumbled, "we could have been snug and safe at

Everleigh already."

Brandon was tired of being reminded. If only *she* had risen earlier that morning, they might have left at the same time as her maid, his valet and the bulk of their luggage, which had probably reached the Norrington's country house hours ago. But he knew recriminations would not improve the situation. "Never fear, we will reach Everleigh yet. If we are a trifle late, I reckon the other guests will be too."

He offered the lady with the spectacles a wry grin. But his next words were aimed at her frosty companion. "We hope not to impose our company upon you for very long. As I recall, there is a coaching inn at Cherhill, which cannot be more than five miles from here. We shall take refuge there until the weather has improved and our carriage can be repaired. May I inquire if you have far to travel?"

The lady gave an anxious nod. "I'm afraid we do. We are bound for Noughtly Hall near Bath, home of the Viscountess of Moresby."

There could be no mistaking the ring of pride in her voice, but her unsociable companion seemed to stiffen even more. Perhaps she was offended by so personal an inquiry. In Brandon's opinion, the unusual circumstances that had thrown them together must permit some relaxation of propriety.

"Are you going to a house party as well?" piped up Imogene, clearly impressed by the other woman's reference to a person of title. Her tone also betrayed a hint of disbelief. Guests invited to such events did not tend to dress so modestly or travel by public stagecoach.

"House party?" The spectacled lady gave a rueful chuckle. "No indeed, we are—"

"We are going for a visit." Her companion turned to fix Brandon with a direct stare that left him gaping and short of breath. "The viscountess is my great-aunt."

"M-miss Cassandra?" It had been four long years since he'd gazed into those compelling dark eyes with their lively flashes of green. Brandon was not prepared for the effect they had upon him. "Or is it *Lady* Cassandra now?"

Perhaps she was known by a different title altogether — one conferred by marriage. Not that it mattered to him in the least.

Her well-shaped chin tilted upward ever so slightly. "I *am* Lady Cassandra. My father survived *his* father long enough to confer that distinction upon my sisters and me."

"Forgive me." Brandon felt himself growing more rattled by the minute, which vexed him. "I have been abroad … with General Wellington's army. I had not heard of your father's death."

During their exchange, Imogene looked from Brandon to Cassandra and back again. The moment their conversation paused, she broke in. "The two of you are acquainted, then? What a small world it is that you should meet again under these circumstances."

A small world? So it was — far too small for Brandon's comfort.

He cursed his ill fortune. Since coming home from his three years of fighting on the Peninsula, he had avoided anywhere he might meet up with Cassandra Whitney. He should have been safe on a country road in winter.

"Lady Cassandra and I were quite well acquainted at one time." As he answered Imogene's question, Brandon endeavored to smooth the bitter edge of his tone.

Four years ago, he had hoped to be even more closely acquainted with the lady. At the time, he had been certain she would welcome such a development. But when he'd summoned the nerve to offer his heart in exchange for her hand, he had discovered she'd only been toying with his affections. How could he have been such a blind fool?

Seeing her again so unexpectedly provoked the surge of painful resentment he'd expected. But he was not prepared for the intense flare of attraction that revived within him as well. If he had any sense, he ought to jump out of the coach and take his chances with the blizzard.

A sharp jab in the ribs from Imogene made Brandon

realize all three women were staring at him expectantly.

"I ... suppose under the circumstances, introductions are in order." He strove to sound calm and controlled. "Imogene, may I present Lady Cassandra Whitney. Lady Cassandra, Imogene Calvert."

As the two women exchanged subdued greetings, Brandon sensed the avid curiosity radiating from Imogene. It was much more difficult to tell how Cassandra might feel. Clearly his skill at guessing the state of her emotions had not improved with time. At least now there was no danger of mistakenly assuming she entertained any affection for him.

Her tone was cool and correct as she returned the introduction. "Allow me to present my travelling companion. Mrs. Davis, Sir Brandon and Lady Calvert."

"*Lady* Calvert?" Imogene burst into tinkling laughter that reminded Brandon of wind rustling through ice-laden tree branches. "No, no, I am not Brandon's wife, only his cousin!"

"Cousin?" At last Cassandra's cool poise appeared shaken. "Forgive me. I assumed ..."

"No need to apologize." Imogene was prepared to be gracious now that she realized Cassandra's connections were more elevated than they appeared. "My dear cousin is certainly in *need* of a wife as I have often reminded him."

"That's quite enough, Imogene!" Brandon chided her, though he was not certain why it flustered him to have his cousin raise the subject of marriage.

"I was only teasing." His cousin shot him a sulky frown. "I'm sure the ladies can see you are quite capable of attracting a wife."

This was getting worse and worse. Brandon wondered how soon they would reach the inn. What must Lady Cassandra think of him, knowing he had remained unwed in the years since his disastrous proposal to her?

With forced heartiness, he sought to steer the conversation in a different direction. "So ... you are going to visit the viscountess? Do you often spend the winter with her?"

Lady Cassandra shook her head. He could not tell whether she welcomed his change of subject or not. "This is my first visit in many years. I am looking forward to it."

She seemed to throw down those words as a challenge, daring Brandon to doubt her.

"Everleigh is not far from Bath," Imogene chirped. "Perhaps we shall see you there if our party ventures into town to attend a concert or an assembly."

"Perhaps." Lady Cassandra did not sound anxious to meet up with them again.

Brandon heartily concurred with that sentiment. It was deucedly awkward being forced into her company again after so many years. And yet … he felt as if this encounter had jolted him fully awake from a long half-sleep.

"Heaven knows when we shall ever reach Bath at this rate." Lady Cassandra cleared away a patch of frost from the window and peered out into the thick-swirling snow. "I believe we could walk faster than the horses are moving."

As if in response to her pronouncement, the plodding stagecoach lurched to a dead halt.

"What now?" Imogene wailed.

"Do not fret." Brandon turned up the collar of his greatcoat and prepared to jam on his hat. "I shall find out what is going on."

He welcomed any diversion from the brittle tension inside the stagecoach.

As he climbed out, his feet sank into snow well past the tops of his riding boots. When the coachman scrambled down from his perch, Brandon gave a violent start. The man was so thickly coated in snow, he scarcely looked human.

"Why have we stopped?" Brandon demanded.

"Do you have to ask?" The driver shot back with a broad sweep of his arm that was almost lost in the impenetrable whiteness around them. "The horses cannot go another step in this or they'll fall dead in their traces, poor beasts."

The alarm that had eased when the stagecoach stopped

to pick up him and his cousin returned with a vengeance. Brandon peered around in every direction, but found it almost impossible to distinguish the sky from the ground. The only thing he could tell with any certainty was that daylight was beginning to fade.

"Could you switch in my carriage horses and let them pull for a bit?"

The coachman shook his head, sending a shower of snow tumbling from his tricorne hat. "They're fine horses, sir, but they haven't the size and strength to pull this great contraption under the best of conditions. I doubt they could budge it a foot in snow this deep. Even if they could, by the time we unharnessed these and put yours in their place, it would be dark."

"What are we to do, then?" Brandon wracked his brain for ideas. "We cannot stay here all night. We would perish!"

His anxiety increased tenfold now that he felt responsible for the safety of *three* women. Hard as he tried to persuade himself that Lady Cassandra Whitney was not his responsibility, his heart refused to heed.

"We could ride my carriage horses," he suggested, "and take shelter at the first house we come to."

The coachman considered Brandon's idea for a long moment before he finally replied. "I reckon it's worth a try, but this is a lonely stretch of road."

He sounded doubtful they would succeed in finding shelter.

Brandon wasn't certain how the venture might turn out either, but he could not sit by and do nothing. Being trapped in close quarters with the woman who had broken his heart while they slowly froze to death was one of the worst endings to his life that he could imagine.

Chapter Two

As Mrs. Davis and Miss Calvert tried to assure one another that all would be well, Cassandra wondered what she had done to deserve this calamity.

Her troublesome conscience was quick to provide an answer. She had refused Sir Brandon Calvert's proposal four years ago after giving every indication that she was smitten with him. She had made a fool of him and perhaps destroyed his faith in women. If that was not bad enough, she had lied to him about her reasons and her feelings, pretending she did not care for him when nothing could have been further from the truth.

If she had cared for him *less*, she might have been able to accept his proposal, concentrating on the benefits to herself rather than the cost to him. As it turned out, the cost might not have been as high as she'd feared. But there was no way she could have known that when Sir Brandon asked her to marry him.

After four long years, during which he had been in her thoughts far too often, seeing him again today had come as a shock ... though not entirely unpleasant. The moment she recognized his deep, melodic voice, Cassandra had wished she could shrink to the size of a mite and crawl into some inconspicuous cranny of the coach box. Since that was impossible, she'd sought to delay the awkward moment when Brandon would recognize *her*.

At first it had seemed possible he might never guess her identity as long as she said nothing and kept her face averted.

But when Mrs. Davis mentioned Aunt Augusta, Cassandra knew she dared not keep silent any longer. If she had, her companion might have divulged the reason for their visit. Cassandra did not want Sir Brandon to learn that she would be acting as a glorified servant to her disagreeable great-aunt. He might despise her for refusing his proposal but she could tolerate his hatred far easier than his pity.

The price for salving her pride had been to face his frank scrutiny and barely-concealed disdain. What had been harder to bear was the agonizing pang when she'd assumed his pretty travelling companion must be his wife.

Over the years, she'd often wondered if he had found a wife capable of returning his bountiful affection without reserve. In magnanimous moments, Cassandra had hoped he would wed a lady who could make him happy and give him the children he yearned for. It was quite another matter to confront the reality of a whining, nagging girl for whom he appeared to feel little more than fond tolerance. Yet how much worse it might have been to see him looking at another woman the way he had once looked at *her*.

Her relief upon learning that he was still unmarried had been so intense Cassandra feared she might humiliate herself by bursting into tears. Fortunately, she had been saved by her pride … and the sudden halt of the stagecoach.

While Sir Brandon went to investigate, she did her best to marshal her composure. She had almost managed when the carriage door opened again and he clambered back inside. Snow clung to his hat and the broad shoulders of his greatcoat. The sculpted planes of his face had been nipped by the winter wind. Somehow, it made the deep, steadfast blue of his eyes gleam all the brighter.

Though he had only been gone a few minutes and Cassandra was prepared for his return, the sight of him still ignited a powerful blaze of awareness within her. Her skin prickled with gooseflesh as if a trickle of melting snow had slithered down her back. Her breath seemed stolen way, as if by a fierce gust of icy wind.

"The snow is too deep," Sir Brandon announced in a ragged, breathless voice. "The horses cannot drag this coach another inch."

"What can we do?" Imogene Calvert demanded in a terror-stricken squeak. "If we stay here, we will freeze to death!"

Her cousin did not try to pacify her with a comforting falsehood, as some men might have done. Instead he gave a grim nod. "That is why we must set out to find shelter before darkness falls. You ladies can ride my carriage horses. The other men and I will lead them on foot."

Before the ladies could respond to his plan, a series of loud knocks thumped on the carriage door. Miss Calvert gave a half-strangled scream.

"The horses must be ready." Sir Brandon inhaled a deep breath and squared his shoulders. "Come now, we haven't a moment to waste."

Pushing the carriage door open again, he climbed out. Cassandra glimpsed the large, sturdy shape of a horse behind him, its chestnut coat glistening with melted snow.

"Come quickly, ladies!" Sir Brandon thrust a hand in.

His cousin cowered back in her seat. Mrs. Davis looked equally reluctant to abandon the dry carriage box for the cold, swirling whiteness outside.

In truth, Cassandra was no more anxious to venture out than they, but it must be done and delay would not make it easier. Perhaps if she set an example, the others would follow. Pulling the hood of her cloak up over her bonnet, she rose and moved to take Sir Brandon's gloved hand.

The wind-driven snow struck her as she emerged from the carriage. An icy blast blew up her skirt, making her shiver and long to retreat back into the relative comfort of the carriage. Fortunately, pride came to her rescue, as it had so often. Whatever else Sir Brandon Calvert might think of her, she refused to appear a coward in his eyes.

So she gritted her teeth against the cold and squinted

     Deborah Hale

against the glare from the snow. She found it easier to ignore those discomforts when she concentrated on Sir Brandon's firm, reliable grasp. Even with the layers of his gloves and hers between their hands, Cassandra sensed heartening warmth radiating from his touch. Dire as their situation might be, she trusted that he would do everything in his power to see her safely through it … in spite of his personal animosity toward her.

Before her feet sank into the snow that came up past his knees, Sir Brandon leaned toward her and raised his voice to carry over the keening wind, "Forgive me for taking this liberty. It cannot be helped."

As she tried to puzzle out what he could mean, Sir Brandon released her hand and slid both of his beneath her cloak to grasp her around the waist. Though he did not squeeze hard, all the air rushed from Cassandra's lungs, just the same. Somehow she retained the presence of mind to brace her hands against his broad shoulders.

The next thing she knew, she was swept upward as if she weighed no more than one of the wafting snowflakes, and deposited on the broad back of a carriage horse. The beast shifted uneasily, not accustomed to bearing a rider. Acting on instinct, Cassandra reached out and gave it a reassuring pat on the neck.

"Are you securely seated?" Sir Brandon inquired. His voice seemed to come from a long distance, even though he still held her around the waist.

"As secure as I can be without a saddle," she called back.

Before her family's fortunes had fallen, she'd been a skilled and intrepid rider. One of the hardest things she'd been obliged to do after her father's death was sell her beautiful thoroughbred mare.

"I'm certain you will manage." In contrast to the warmth and care his touch conveyed, the baronet's voice sounded as fierce and icy as the gusts sweeping over the Wiltshire Downs.

He wrenched his hands away from her and turned back

to the stagecoach. A whimper broke from Cassandra's lips. It felt as if his fingers had been frozen to her flesh and ripped away bits of it when he removed them. Fortunately the high-pitched howl of the wind whipped the sound away before anyone else could hear.

Ordering herself not to be so foolish, she threaded the gloved fingers of one hand through the coarse hair of the horse's mane. With the other, she tugged her cloak closed as best she could against the elements. Through the fast-falling snow, she could make out the shapes of the other passengers being helped down from the coach.

Then she heard voices raised loud enough to pierce the shriek of the storm. "Don't be ridiculous, Imogene! You *must* come. The driver assures me we are no more than a mile from shelter."

"Then go find it and come back to fetch me." Miss Calvert cried in a voice sharp with panic.

"Who knows if we *could* find you again in this?" Her cousin seemed to be fast losing patience. "We must stay together! It is our best hope. We cannot afford to delay!"

"But it's cold out there." The lady continued to resist. "What if we get lost?"

"Do come, Miss Calvert!" Cassandra called during a lull in their argument. "You can ride with me. It will be an adventure!"

She was not certain her appeal would work but it was all she could think of at the moment. Sir Brandon was right — they could not afford to wait any longer. But neither could they leave his stubbornly terrified cousin behind to freeze.

Perhaps her coaxing worked or perhaps Sir Brandon took advantage of the momentary distraction to seize his cousin and hoist her up behind Cassandra. Miss Calvert gave a ter-rified scream which Cassandra feared might spook the horse. Luckily, the creature was too tired or too miserable to care.

"What if I fall off?" she squeaked.

"It will be a soft landing in the snow," her cousin snapped.

"Then you shall have to walk. So I suggest you make an effort to keep your seat."

"Hold on to me," Cassandra urged the girl. "I have a good grip on the horse's mane."

Not good enough to keep them both from sliding off the beast's back if it moved at anything faster than a sedate walk. But she had no intention of betraying her doubts to Imogene Calvert.

The lady's fear overcame any reservations about being too familiar. Miss Calvert threw her arms around Cassandra's waist and locked them there by stuffing her hands into either end of her fur muff.

When the horse took a lurching step forward, Imogene Calvert emitted a choked cry and plastered herself tight against Cassandra's back. At least it provided a little warmth, as did the body of the horse beneath her. She would have given anything for a hot brick under her icy feet, however.

The driving snow stung her face like an endless series of pin pricks. Her nose began to run but she did not dare relax her hold on the horse's mane to wipe it. Instead, she sniffed as quietly as she could, hoping Sir Brandon would not hear and assume she was weeping.

As the snow swirled around them and darkness descended, Cassandra prayed they would not stray from the road. If they did, their party might wander in the empty downland until they all perished. Though she could no longer make out the shape of Sir Brandon leading the horse, she heard him now and then address an encouraging word to the creature. Even when he did not speak, she sensed his presence and took courage from it.

They could not have met again under worse circumstances. Relations between them could never be anything but strained and awkward. Yet part of her still warmed with gratitude to have seen and spoken to him again after all this time. Even if she dared not tell him any of the things that were in her heart.

Was Lady Cassandra Whitney as brave as she seemed?

Brandon mulled over that question as he trudged through the deep snow in the fast-fading light. Or was she simply too proud to show her fear?

If the latter, then her behavior was a form of deception — something he had long abhorred. He'd grown up in a family where appearance was all that signified no matter what corruption festered beneath the carefully cultivated surface.

He would never have blamed the lady for rejecting his proposal. That was her prerogative after all and the dukes of Norland were considerably above a mere baronet, no matter how great his fortune. What offended him was that Lady Cassandra had misled him about her feelings, giving him false hope of winning her.

Fuelled by the heat of righteous indignation, Brandon's pace sped up and he became far less conscious of the biting cold.

"How much farther must we go?" Imogene wailed. "Are you sure we are still on the road?"

His cousin's questions jolted Brandon back to their present predicament with jarring abruptness. Could he answer either one truthfully without reducing Imogene to a state of frenzied panic?

Before he could contrive a way to satisfy both his compulsive honesty and the practical demands of the situation, Lady Cassandra answered his cousin in a soothing tone. "We must be a good deal nearer to some place of shelter than we were when we set out. I am certain we are still on the road. I can just make out a hedgerow to our right. Can you?"

After an uncertain pause, Imogene replied, "I believe I can. Yes I can. Oh, thank heaven!"

Silently Brandon echoed that sentiment. As long as they followed the hedgerow, it would keep them on the road which would eventually lead to some habitation, even at their present plodding pace.

For a moment he forgot the anguish he had suffered at the hands of Lady Cassandra Whitney. Instead he could have kissed her for calming his cousin and reviving his spirits. Even if she acted braver than she truly felt, perhaps that was not such an inexcusable deception under the circumstances. Hadn't he done the same in Spain before a battle to keep up the morale of his men?

The spark of hope Lady Cassandra had kindled burst into full flame a short while later when Brandon heard the distant bark of a dog over the howling wind. He squinted in the direction of the sound and glimpsed a faint, diffuse light through the thick curtain of blowing snow.

"Lights!" he cried. "Call back to the others!"

Imogene and Lady Cassandra were eager to oblige. Behind him, Brandon heard the echo of his words as they were passed down the column.

"Come on, old fellow," he urged the horse, tugging it toward the light and the barking dog, "only a little farther, then you will be able to rest somewhere warm and dry."

Whatever this place was, they would seek shelter for the night and he would pay handsomely for their hospitality. Tomorrow, after the storm passed, he would dispatch a blacksmith to repair his carriage. Then he and Imogene would continue on their journey while Lady Cassandra went her own way. With luck, he would not lay eyes on her again for a great many more years. Perhaps by then he might master the skill of being near her while remaining unaffected.

The horse blew out its breath in what sounded like a sigh of relief. Its steps hastened as if it understood that it would soon be able to rest and eat.

The dog continued to bark, for which Brandon blessed it. The nearer they drew to the sound, the better he could make out the light thrown by candles in the windows of a house. Though it was difficult to judge the size of the place in the gathering darkness, through the blur of snow, he sensed it was not large. It must be a farmhouse or laborer's cottage. As long as the place had a roof, four walls and a hearth, it would suffice for the night.

Just then another light appeared, bobbing toward them in the darkness. Brandon heard a deep voice boom out. "Hush, Podger! Go lay down you daft whelp, before you wake the dead."

"Hullo?" Brandon called when the dog quieted as its master bid. "I beg your pardon for the disturbance."

"Don't bother about that," replied a well-muffled man, who approached them bearing a lantern. "I reckon you didn't have much choice. Caught on the road by the storm, were you?"

"We were, indeed." Brandon continued moving toward the man, for he feared it might be impossible to budge the horse again if they stopped. "If it would not be too great an imposition, might our party seek shelter here for the night? We shall be happy to pay you for your trouble."

"Don't bother about that either." The man beckoned them forward with a wide sweep of his arm. "Never let it be said Tobias Martin turned away folk who needed his hospitality. How many in your party?"

Brandon did a quick mental count.

"Eight," he replied in an apologetic tone, "and six horses. If that is more than you can accommodate perhaps you would be kind enough to tell us how far it is to the next village."

"More than half a mile to Cherhill," Mr. Martin replied. "Not but a step in fair weather. Heaven knows how long it would take on a night like this. I hardly trust myself not to go astray betwixt my house and barn. It'll be a squeeze, I reckon, but you're welcome to stay with us as long as you need."

"We shall be very much obliged to you, Mr. Martin." Brandon could tell he would like this bluff, honest countryman who had offered them hospitality without even knowing their names. "I hope we shall not have to impose upon you more than one night."

By now they had reached the barn. The warm, pungent smells of hay and livestock were perfume to Brandon's nose after the freezing, scentless trek through the storm.

He brought the horse to a halt then trudged back and raised his arms to his cousin. "Down you get, Imogene. Aren't you glad you came with us now?"

"That remains to be seen." She pried her arms from around Lady Cassandra and let Brandon lift her down.

Her earlier panic seemed to have dissipated, for which he was grateful. But in its place he sensed her ridiculous haughtiness returning. Brandon would have welcomed some middle ground.

He was pleased that she lowered her voice before demanding. "What is this place? Could we not press on to find a proper inn?"

"No, we could not." He set her on her feet harder than he'd intended. "We were fortunate to find a hospitable welcome here. Show a little gratitude."

He let his cousin go and turned to assist Lady Cassandra, only to find she had already begun to slide off the horse's back. Was she trying to avoid further contact with him after he'd seized hold of her earlier? Or was she too chilled and weary to keep her seat?

Whatever the reason, Brandon's instincts took over. He caught her in his arms and eased her the rest of the way to the ground.

"Are you alright?" he asked in an anxious tone he wished he could disguise.

As one arm continued to support her, he raised his other hand and brushed away some of the snow that had accumulated on her hood. Heaven help him, the gesture was almost a caress.

"I am quite well, thank you." The breathless quality of her voice contradicted her words. "At least I shall be once I thaw out. Excuse me. I must find out how Mrs. Davis fared on our excursion."

Brandon had no choice but to let her go, which he told himself should come as a relief. Yet it did not feel that way.

"Thank you," he said before she moved out of earshot, "for keeping Imogene calm. I wish I had your knack for it."

"No need to thank me." She lingered near him for a tantalizing instant. "It was the least I could do."

What did she mean by that? Brandon wondered as Mr. Martin ushered the ladies into the house with rustic gentility, while he helped the other men unharness and tend to the weary horses. Did Lady Cassandra feel some remorse for the injury she'd once done him and seek to atone for it? Brandon was not sure he wanted that, or anything else that might threaten to rekindle feelings he had struggled so long to subdue.

Chapter Three

THERE HAD BEEN times since they set out from the stranded stagecoach that Cassandra had feared Imogene Calvert might squeeze the life out of her or perhaps send them both tumbling off the horse into the snow. The girl's bleats of fright every time the creature took a step rubbed Cassandra's nerves raw. Still she had managed to keep her temper and do everything in her power to soothe Miss Calvert.

After all, she *had* invited Sir Brandon's cousin to ride with her and she knew their situation would only be made worse if Miss Calvert lost her nerve altogether. But the chief reason she'd remained patient with the girl was her need to make amends in some small way for the humiliation she had caused Sir Brandon. It made her feel a bit less beholden to her former suitor.

Now, as the kind farmer led her and the other ladies into the thatched-roofed cottage, Cassandra strove to dismiss the sensations that had overwhelmed her when Sir Brandon caught her in his arms and eased her to the ground. She had no business feeling buoyant and light-headed. There was no excuse for her intense inclination to linger near him.

"Welcome to our humble home, ladies," Mr. Martin ushered them into a narrow entry hall where several coats and cloaks hung from pegs on both walls. "I reckon you are accustomed to finer lodgings than this, but any port in a storm is better than none, as they say."

Before they could reply, he called out, "Come greet our guests, Mother! Their carriages got stuck in the snow so they are going to stop with us for a spell. If this storm keeps up, who knows but we may have company for Twelfth Night."

"Oh no!" Miss Calvert cried. "Surely we will not be stranded here that long!"

If one of her sisters had uttered such a tactless remark, Cassandra would have swiftly silenced her with a firm nudge in the ribs. But she could hardly do that to Sir Brandon's cousin, whom she had met only hours ago. Instead she did her best to make it sound more courteous. "Of course we hope we shall not be obliged to trespass on your hospitality that long, sir. It is kind of you to speak as if our presence would be a pleasure rather than a burden."

"Very kind, indeed," Mrs. Davis murmured in support.

Just then a plump little woman appeared, wiping her hands on her apron. Wisps of ginger hair curled out from beneath her cap. "Well, well, didn't I say there would be travelers stranded on the road with this storm coming on so sudden? Welcome, my dears. Hang up your wraps and come through to the parlor to warm yourselves. I've a good fire going and the kettle is on for tea."

"Thank you, Mrs. Martin," Cassandra replied before Imogene Calvert had a chance to speak. "You are a gracious hostess. We were fortunate indeed to find our way to your house."

She removed her snow-covered cloak then peeled off her gloves and untied the ribbons of her bonnet with stiff, uncooperative fingers. By the time she and the others hung up their wraps, the men had begun to enter behind them. At the urging of their hostess, the three women followed her into the parlor.

The room was less than half the size of the smallest sitting room in the ducal mansion where Cassandra had resided so briefly. She hoped Sir Brandon would not bump his head on one of the sturdy wooden beams that protruded from the low ceiling. But the parlor's modest dimensions made it far cozier on a stormy winter night, especially with a cheery fire blazing in the wide stone hearth.

Several plain, solid chairs clustered around the walls facing the fire. A wide seat had been hewn into the thick outer wall of the house beneath a pair of small, shuttered windows. Cassandra and Mrs. Davis sank down on it together while Imogene Calvert selected the chair nearest to the fire and perched there. She surveyed the Martins' snug parlor with barely concealed disdain.

Fortunately Mrs. Martin did not appear to notice. She stood beside the hearth beaming at her guests. "I fear you have me at a disadvantage, ladies. You know my name but I do not know yours. I reckon introductions are in order, don't you?"

"I do indeed, ma'am," Cassandra replied, rubbing her hands together to relieve the painful prickling as they began to warm. "I am Cassandra Whitney. This is my friend Mrs. Davis and Miss Calvert, whom we met on the road today."

She explained how the Calvert's carriage broke down and its occupants had been picked up by the stagecoach, which later got stuck in the snow.

"That is more adventure than I should care to have in a whole year." Mrs. Martin shook her head over their predicament. "Though I suppose it will make an exciting story to tell, Miss Whitney. Or is it Miss Cassandra?"

She was referring to the custom for the eldest daughter of a family to be addressed by her surname while younger ones were known by their given names.

Cassandra was about to reply when Imogene Calvert spoke up. "It is *Lady* Cassandra, in fact. Her father was the Duke of Norland."

Inwardly, Cassandra cringed at Miss Calvert's lofty tone. She was in no position to exult over anyone, least of all their hosts, who were behaving more graciously than many persons of title she could name.

"Lady Cassandra?" Mrs. Martin repeated with evident relish. "Well, fancy that. I never expected to entertain a duke's daughter!"

"I am more apt to answer to Miss Cassandra." She attempted to make light of the whole question. "That is how I was known for most of my life. I feel quite a fraud using any title since my father held his for such a short time before it passed to his cousin."

She welcomed the arrival of the men, hoping their presence would bring a change of conversation. The stagecoach driver and the Calvert's coachman entered first, followed by two younger men. One was the coach guard, while the other Cassandra assumed to be the Calvert's footman.

By the time Sir Brandon entered, blowing on his fingers to warm them, all the chairs in the Martins' parlor were occupied. The young footman started to vacate his seat for his master but Mrs. Martin had other ideas.

"There is room on the window seat, sir, if the ladies do not mind budging up a bit." She did not wait to hear if they objected, but practically dragged the baronet over and pushed him down beside Cassandra.

Thank heaven she had been out in the cold so long! Her cheeks were already bright red, which would conceal the furious blush that rose in them now.

With his usual courtesy Sir Brandon thanked their hostess when Cassandra knew he must want to do quite the opposite. She budged up as far as she could without doing poor Mrs. Davis an injury, yet her right leg still pressed against the baronet's, a familiarity of which she was far too aware.

He did not appear to notice. Instead he introduced himself and the other men to their hosts.

"A pleasure, I'm sure," declared the lady of the house with obvious sincerity. "Now you all need a good hot drink to warm you up. If you'll excuse me, I shall go make the tea."

Mr. Martin raised one large hand to stay her. "I reckon these folks need something a mite stronger than tea, Mother. Have we any of that mulled cider left from Christmas?"

"Plenty, my dear!" Mrs. Martin beamed at her husband's cleverness. "I have no doubt that will soon revive them, poor frozen souls."

In spite of Cassandra's discomfort at being forced into such close contact with her former suitor, she could not help but notice the easy affection between Mr. and Mrs. Martin. She envied it. No doubt they had fancied one another in their younger years and wed for that reason alone. It was a luxury she and her sisters had never been permitted. Now it was too late, except perhaps for Evie. She hoped her sister would marry for love and not feel bound to accept an uncongenial suitor simply because he could improve her family's fortunes.

That thought made Cassandra even more conscious of the gentleman she had once hoped to marry for love. Her nostrils tingled at the faint tang of his shaving soap, so familiar to her even after all this time. More than the sight of him, the sound of his voice or even the disconcerting physical contact between them, that scent transported her back to her first Season in London. It threatened to revive the emotions she had experienced then with painful intensity.

As Mrs. Martin headed off to fetch refreshments, Cassandra scrambled to her feet and followed.

"Let me help you." Her offer came out in the tone of a desperate plea.

"No need for that, my dear." Mrs. Martin tried to wave her back but Cassandra held her ground. She would rather have her feet put to the fire than go back and squeeze in so close to a man who must despise her, as Sir Brandon Calvert had every right to do.

"I gave our chore girl a little holiday to visit her family in Avebury," Mrs. Martin admitted, "but I can manage. You are our guest and the daughter of a duke."

"If you think that will make me a hindrance in your kitchen," Cassandra persisted, "I can assure you I am no stranger to housework. I like to make myself useful and I expect I will warm up faster by moving around than by sitting still."

As they spoke, the two women made their way down a

narrow passage that opened into a tidy kitchen. A large cooking hearth mirrored the one in the parlor. A good fire burned in it while a copper kettle whistled on the hob.

Mrs. Martin turned to fix Cassandra with a puzzled look.

"Is it that young gentleman?" She lowered her voice so as not to carry back to the parlor where the others had begun to talk among themselves. "Was I wrong to seat him beside you? He is a handsome fellow, but they are not always the most agreeable."

Cassandra knew she should not betray anything of her feelings toward Sir Brandon. Especially not to a woman she had just met. Yet she could not allow anyone to speak ill of him and go unchallenged. "I have known gentlemen like that, but Sir Brandon Calvert is not one of them. If anything, his character is more agreeable than his looks."

"I see." Mrs. Martin began bustling about her kitchen. "So you have met him before? Can I trouble you to fetch those cups down from the shelf?"

Cassandra turned to the task, grateful for any diversion. "I was once acquainted with him but I fear we did not part on the best of terms. The fault for that is entirely mine. I would rather not subject him to my company any more than our circumstances make necessary."

"Are you certain he is still angry with you?" Mrs. Martin inquired as casually as she might have asked about the weather.

"Quite certain." Cassandra insisted as she took the last of the cups down. She did not want their hostess to get any ridiculous ideas about her and Sir Brandon any more than she wanted to. That would only lead to more heartache — something she had suffered enough to last a lifetime.

"I hope you will be able to keep your distance from the gentleman if that is your wish, my dear." Mrs. Martin sounded doubtful. "But that is a lot of snow outside and this is not a very big house."

❄

It appeared Lady Cassandra's attitude toward him had not thawed after all.

As Brandon wrapped his hands around the warm cup and sipped its spicy-sweet contents, he told himself he would not wish it any other way. When she had leapt from her place beside him to assist their hostess, a sense of relief had surged through him. Now he would not have to work so hard to ignore her when all his senses fairly screamed their awareness of her leg pressed against his.

At the same time, a sharp pain pierced his chest, chilling in its intensity. It contradicted the wishful belief he'd cultivated in recent years that Cassandra Whitney no longer meant anything to him.

He told himself not to be ridiculous. He was no longer a green, young fool in the throes of his first love. He had gone to war, where he'd taken lives and nearly lost his on more than one occasion. After four years he thought he had forgotten Cassandra Whitney. But seeing her again, so unexpectedly, brought back memories of their old courtship, as fresh as if it had been yesterday. It was the years and experiences since then that felt like a hazy dream he could scarcely recall.

The stagecoach driver took a deep swig of his cider then nodded toward the window. "That is the worst snow I've seen this far south in all my years driving this route."

Mr. Martin nodded. "The winters are growing colder than when I were a lad."

The two men began recalling previous snowy winters, sometimes arguing good-naturedly about the precise year, with Brandon's coachman acting as a sort of referee. The others listened, sipping their cider. Now and then one would venture a remark. Imogene sat by the fire with a stiff posture and an expression that proclaimed her desire to be somewhere else.

Brandon could sympathize with her feelings to a point. Given a choice, he would rather not have been cooped up in a small house with the woman who'd once broken his heart.

However, as with many events in life, he had not been given a choice. All he could do was remind himself how much worse the situation might have been. What could not be avoided must be endured with as much grace as one could muster.

Perhaps the years had taught Lady Cassandra that same lesson. He could not help but contrast her behavior with his cousin's. Though he was certain she had only offered to assist their hostess in order to get away from him, he could not help but approve her obliging manner.

Now she returned to the parlor, following Mrs. Martin. Brandon schooled his expression to one of cool indifference. He pretended not to notice the brisk grace of her movements or the quiet, capable way she helped out their hostess as if she were accustomed to such domestic tasks.

Carrying a stack of plates and cutlery, Mrs. Martin made a circuit of the room, dispensing them to the guests. Lady Cassandra went behind her with a tray of cold meats.

"Help yourselves, everyone," their hostess urged. "There is plenty in the larder, so don't be delicate."

Brandon had no intention of being delicate. Breakfast had been many hours ago and trudging through the deep snow had sharpened his appetite further. But when Lady Cassandra held the tray out to him, he struggled to ignore her as resolutely as she did him.

He did not bother surveying the contents of the plate for the largest or choicest pieces but took the first one he could spear with a fork. He did not want Lady Cassandra lingering near him where he might be drawn to notice her elegant long-fingered hands or experience a foolish rush of relief that she wore no rings on any of them.

The moment he murmured a stiff "thank you" she moved on, with a palpable air of relief, to serve Mrs. Davis.

Brandon took a bite of his meat and discovered it was cold roast pork. He could not imagine any of the dainty refreshments at Everleigh tasting so good. He only wished he had not let Lady Cassandra distract him from taking a larger helping.

Now that she was no longer standing in front of him, he did not feel obliged to keep his eyes off her. He permitted his gaze to followed her as she moved around the room with her tray. She looked taller than he remembered, or perhaps she only seemed that way compared to their diminutive hostess. Her figure still retained its youthful slenderness. The firelight brought out rich chestnut glints in her dark hair, which the damp air had teased into curls.

Once she moved away from him, her bearing seemed to relax. She exchanged a few words with each of the other men as she served them. Brandon dismissed a pang which was most definitely not envy.

Later, when Lady Cassandra came around with a platter of cheese, he took more time making his selection so she would have an opportunity to speak to him if she chose. Instead, she stood frozen like a statue of ice until he finished. When he tried to meet her gaze, he found it fixed on a point above his head. Had he only imagined her regretful murmur when he'd helped her down from the horse? Or had her relief over their narrow escape from disaster made her forget herself?

He did not care how she behaved toward him or why! Brandon snatched up several pieces of cheese with fierce abruptness which made Lady Cassandra flinch. All that mattered was getting through their stay at the Martin farm until they could go their separate ways. The situation could not be avoided, but surely they could endure it with more grace.

Just then Lady Cassandra glanced down and caught him staring at her. Brandon started as if he's been discovered committing a crime, while she turned and hurried back to the kitchen without serving his cousin.

Most of the others were busy eating with brief pauses to praise Mrs. Martin's cooking. Brandon set down his plate on the window seat and slipped away to the kitchen. He found Cassandra staring out the window, so lost in thought that she did not seem to hear him enter.

"It cannot keep on like this you know." He meant to

reassure her, but instead his words came out in a gruff mutter.

She spun around to face him with the defensive air of one who had been ambushed. "We cannot keep on like *what*?"

Brandon shook his head. "That was not what I said. I was referring to the weather. The snow will likely stop during the night, or else change to rain and melt much of what has fallen already. Then we shall be able to rescue our stranded vehicles and be on our way."

That was what he wanted — to get away as soon as possible from Lady Cassandra Whitney and the memories their meeting had revived. Then he and Imogene would join the house party at Everleigh where he would seek an opportunity to propose to Miss Reynolds, a lady he had decided would make him a good, loyal wife. With luck, by this time next winter they might be expecting the birth of an heir to keep the family title in the hands of true Calvert descendants.

"I must have misheard you." Lady Cassandra's tone dared him to question her mistake. "No doubt you are correct about the weather."

Brandon could not allow such an opportunity to pass without taking advantage of it. "Perhaps *we* should not go on as we have been either. This house is altogether too small to let us each behave as if the other is invisible. What were you thinking just now — that you would rather be snowbound with any man in the world other than me?"

"I was thinking no such thing!" Like Hamlet's Ophelia, she protested too much for Brandon to believe.

He arched one eyebrow and fixed her with a penetrating gaze. "The truth, if you please. The past four years have not made me any more inclined to abide deception."

"There is a difference between deception and discretion you know." Lady Cassandra scowled — an expression that would have looked unattractive on any other woman. Somehow she contrived to make it appear charming.

"Very well!" she admitted. "It was rather a shock to see you again after all this time and more than a little awkward considering how we parted. I am certain it cannot have been an agreeable experience for you either."

How could he deny it after insisting on the truth from her? Perhaps Lady Cassandra had a point about deception and discretion. Brandon did not care to admit that meeting her again dismayed him, for that would suggest feelings of hurt and betrayal he should have put behind him long ago.

But he would far rather own to such feelings than to the perverse flashes of pleasure their inconvenient reunion provoked in him. "Of course our meeting was a surprise for me as well. And being thrown together like this in such close quarters is, as you say, rather … awkward."

The lady's defensive scowl eased.

"But it does not need to be," Brandon ventured. "Whatever else we may think of one another, surely we can agree we are both sensible people."

Somehow, he did not feel as sensible as before he'd laid eyes on her again.

Lady Cassandra gave a cautious nod.

Heartened, Brandon continued, "Two sensible people should be capable of putting the past behind them and getting on together for a little while, don't you agree?"

She did not avoid his gaze now but met it directly, as if it were a challenge. "I can if you can."

A chill trickled down Brandon's spine, unsettling yet strangely stimulating. "I am not proposing a contest, but a truce. For as long as we are forced to remain in this house, let us endeavor to treat each other as brand new acquaintances."

Lady Cassandra squared her shoulders and tilted her chin. "Agreed. As you say, we will likely go our separate ways in the morning."

Though that was precisely what Brandon hoped, her reminder troubled him. He brushed such feelings aside and swept a glance around the kitchen, with its dark wooden floor, beam and plaster walls and massive cooking hearth. "Is there anything I can do to help?"

Her plucky assistance to Mrs. Martin made him feel idle by comparison, even though he knew she had only been trying to get away from him. Besides, he needed some excuse for following her to the kitchen, in case anyone noticed.

"You could take in that plate of cake." Lady Cassandra nodded toward the table where it sat.

Without another word, Brandon picked up the well-laden plate and headed back to the parlor. He told himself he might be better off for having to spend time with Cassandra Whitney again. Their encounter might finally allow him to close that chapter of his life and begin a new one with Isabella Reynolds.

Chapter Four

No doubt Sir Brandon was right. Cassandra gazed after him as he headed back to the parlor bearing the plate of cake. The weather would clear by morning and they would go their separate ways. Until then, they should make every effort to forget the past and treat each other with as much civility as possible.

It surprised her a little and relieved her mind a great deal that he had suggested they behave in such a rational manner. She had feared he might still hate her for the way she'd treated him. She had worried he might raise the painful subject of their past or inquire too closely about her present circumstances.

An oppressive weight seemed to slip from her shoulders as she realized she had been anxious for no reason. She should have known Sir Brandon Calvert would not hold her refusal against her all this time. Perhaps he had never cared for her as much as she'd once believed. Or perhaps, with time and experience, he had come to realize they might not have made a compatible match after all.

Those thoughts should have brought her more comfort than they did.

Cassandra seized the tray of cheese she had set on the sideboard and followed Sir Brandon back to the parlor. Activity and company were what she needed to divert her from such fruitless speculation.

She entered the parlor just in time to hear Mrs. Martin ask, "Where were you bound for, before the storm stranded you here?"

Miss Calvert was quick to reply, though Cassandra was not certain the question had been addressed to her. "My cousin and I are on our way to a house party at Everleigh, the estate of Lord and Lady Norrington, just beyond Bath. My maid went on ahead of us, with most of my luggage. What shall I do without her? Where will I sleep?"

If Mrs. Martin resented Miss Calvert's tone, she was too good-natured to let it show. "You ladies are welcome to the room where our daughters used to sleep. The chore girl uses it now, but the bed is big enough for three in a pinch. It is fortunate you are all so slender."

Miss Calvert's grimace made it clear she was not accustomed to sharing a bed.

"Imogene," her cousin murmured in a low, warning tone, "we are blessed to be warm and dry with a roof over our heads. I shall be content to sleep in a chair or on the floor. Either would be infinitely preferable to a freezing coachbox."

"That is true," Miss Calvert acknowledged with a sigh. "But how am I to manage without Williams to look after me? After this, I shall always keep her with me when I travel."

Cassandra caught Mrs. Davis's eye. She sensed they were both thinking the same thing. Clearly Miss Calvert did not appreciate how fortunate she was to *have* a lady's maid. It was a luxury Cassandra and her sisters had long since learned to do without. Though the others missed such service, Cassandra had learned to value her hard-won self-reliance.

"Whatever assistance you require," she assured the young lady, "I shall be happy to provide it."

Miss Calvert looked rather shocked by her offer. "That is kind of you, Lady Cassandra, but I could not impose upon the daughter of a duke!"

Did the young lady realize how little that distinction signified without the fortune that usually accompanied it? "My late father's title did not prevent me from acquiring a few useful skills which come in handy at times like these. I should be pleased to place them at your disposal."

Cassandra tried not to notice the look of gratitude Sir Brandon directed her way. He must think she was being gracious by offering to assist his cousin. Her conscience protested that she did not deserve him to think well of her.

"Were you ladies on your way to that house party as well?" asked Mrs. Martin.

Cassandra shook her head. "Mrs. Davis and I were headed to visit my great-aunt who lives near Bath."

"The Viscountess of Moresby," Miss Calvert informed their hosts who looked suitably impressed.

Their reaction brought Cassandra's conscience another pang. If Sir Brandon knew the true circumstances of her visit to Noughtly Hall, he might accuse her of deception, but she did not see it that way. After tomorrow, it was unlikely she would encounter any of these people again. Why should they know the particulars of her situation? Were she and her family not entitled to a little privacy?

Once the travelers had thawed out and eaten their fill, they began to converse in groups around the parlor. Mrs. Davis and Mrs. Martin discovered they had some mutual acquaintances from their youth, which gave them plenty to talk about. The men seemed to share a particular interest in horses. They were soon exchanging stories about the fastest, strongest and worst-tempered beasts they had known.

Imogene Calvert cornered Cassandra on the window seat and proceeded to regale her with every detail of her Season in London the previous spring. Cassandra tried to appear interested in the subject as she strove to prevent her gaze from wandering in the direction of Sir Brandon.

That was not an easy task. From the moment they had been first introduced at a ball hosted by the Countess of Penryn, she'd found her attention continually drawn to him whenever they were together. It was not only his stature, lithe build and striking features that attracted her, though she could not deny their appeal. Sir Brandon also possessed an air of integrity she could not help but admire. She had sensed he valued her for more than her looks or family connections. He clearly approved of her strong will and independent spirit in a way few other men did. Each of them had challenged the other and relished that challenge.

Out of the corner of her eye, Cassandra saw Sir Brandon rise from his place among the men. Hard as she tried to focus her full attention on his cousin, her pulse began to race and her flesh buzzed with heightened awareness as he strolled toward them.

The intervening years had done nothing to make him *less* attractive — quite the contrary. His features had grown sharper and bolder, his bearing more assured. No doubt his military service had challenged him in a way no woman ever could. Cassandra was certain he had risen to the challenge admirably.

If only they *were* meeting for the first time today, as he had asked her to pretend, without the troubles of the past to spoil their acquaintance …

What then? Reason demanded. Even if they had never met before, how could she begin to compete for his attention against so many ladies in Society who were younger and more vivacious? Ladies who possessed generous dowries and were not encumbered with family responsibilities? Even if, by some miracle, he did prefer her to all of them, how could she agree to a union where all the advantage would accrue to her, with nothing but burdens upon him?

In spite of those considerations, when Brandon Calvert sank onto the window seat beside his cousin, Cassandra's heart seemed to quiver in her chest rather than beat.

"I hope you ladies do not object to my company." He lowered his voice to a conspiratorial murmur that fell on Cassandra's ears like a secret caress. "I admire a fine horse as much as the next man, but I can only converse about the creatures for so long. *Any* other subject would be most diverting."

"Lady Cassandra and I were talking about London," his cousin informed him. "She hopes to bring her youngest sister out for the Season."

"If not this year, then certainly next." Cassandra's gaze faltered before Sir Brandon's. "Perhaps by then the war will be over and there will be a bumper crop of returning officers seeking wives."

No sooner had the words left her mouth than she wished she could take them back.

"Like my cousin." Miss Calvert gave a trill of high-pitched laughter. "He is fortunate to have resigned his commission early and beat the rush. But you must not count on him as a suitor for your sister. If I have any influence in the matter, he will be married well before she makes her debut."

Cassandra struggled to hide her dismay. She reminded herself that she wanted Brandon to be happy in the way a loving wife and family could make him. Yet the thought of him belonging to another woman gnawed at her heart. The notion of having him as the husband of her beloved younger sister threatened a lifetime of grief she could not bear to contemplate.

In response to his cousin's remark, Sir Brandon's handsome mouth tightened. "I do not need anyone matchmaking on my behalf, Imogene."

Was he referring to *her* as well? Cassandra resented the notion. Did he suppose for one moment she would push her sister at him after having previously refused his offer of marriage?

Perhaps Sir Brandon repented his severity, for he seemed to make an effort to moderate his tone. "I shall be the one trying to find *you* a suitable husband among the gentlemen at Everleigh, as I promised your mother I would."

Miss Calvert wrinkled her delicate nose. "I wish your idea of a suitable husband was closer to mine."

"There is more to a good match than a title, a fortune and a handsome face," her cousin insisted. "Don't you agree, Lady Cassandra?"

If he had doused her with a pitcher of ice water, he could not have caught Cassandra off-guard any worse.

"I ... er ..." she sputtered, vexed with him for putting her on the spot. Was this his idea of behaving like new acquaintances? "Having never been married, I am hardly qualified to offer an opinion."

She concluded her reply with a faint note of triumph. She had managed to evade the verbal trap Sir Brandon had set for her. However, if she expected him to let her off so easily, Cassandra soon realized she was mistaken.

"A very diplomatic answer." His blue eyes flashed with good-natured mockery. "You were not always so judicious with your opinions on any subject, regardless of your personal experience."

"Perhaps I have grown more prudent with my advancing years," she quipped back. This reminded her of the way they had once bantered during their courtship.

"That would be a pity. Your boldness was one of the things I always admired about you." Sir Brandon's lips arched into a half-smile which had a sweetly devastating effect upon Cassandra.

It made her want to shove his cousin out of the way, lunge at him across the window seat and kiss him breathless.

Fortunately, Imogene Calvert broke in on their exchange before Cassandra lost her head entirely. The girl sounded vexed that they were not paying sufficient attention to her. "I expect Lady Cassandra agrees with me, but does not wish to offend you, dear Bran. A man like Lord Alanham, with a fortune, a title and good looks would make a splendid catch. I cannot think why you do not approve of him."

Cassandra's gaze flew to lock with Sir Brandon's. She recalled Lord Alanham from her time in London Society. Did poor Miranda still secretly pine for *her* former suitor the way Cassandra had for hers?

Lord Alanham? The mere mention of that name drove the beginning of a smile from Brandon's face, as if he had bitten into an apple and found it full of worms.

When he detected a flicker of recognition in Cassandra's dark eyes, his features settled into a scowl. Prior to her unexpected rejection of his proposal, the only point of friction between them had been his persistent disapproval of her sister's suitor.

In response to Imogene and Cassandra's stares, he muttered something vague about not judging a book by its cover.

Every lady of their acquaintance considered Lord Alanham perfectly charming, just as all their schoolmasters once had. But Brandon had glimpsed another side of his old schoolmate. As a consequence, he would never trust the fellow. But honor forbade him to tarnish the reputation of even his worst enemy without solid evidence of wrongdoing.

Could it be his antagonism toward such a seemingly agreeable gentleman that had soured Lady Cassandra's feelings for him? If so, it increased his dislike of Alanham even further.

He braced for her to join his cousin in defending the fellow.

"Social standing and financial security are advantages any sensible woman must consider when she contemplates marriage." Lady Cassandra's tone sounded defensive. "And a handsome face is not to be sneered at."

Brandon had expected her to offer just such an opinion. Yet that did not diminish the sting of hearing her praise a man he detested. He prepared to contradict her.

But before he could summon the words, Lady Cassandra continued, "However one must not forget that position and wealth can be lost and time will take its toll on even the handsomest face. A kind heart and honorable character are advantages that will last and even improve with age."

Brandon's jaw fell slack, though perhaps that was better than grinning like a fool.

"Forgive me, Miss Calvert!" Lady Cassandra's attractive features twisted into a rueful grimace. "I did not mean to subject you to a sermon or a lecture. It seems I am still as opinionated as your cousin accused me of being, even when I have no experience upon which to base my beliefs."

"I did not accuse you!" Brandon protested, though he sensed she was only teasing. "I reckon your opinion is a very sound one."

"Of course you do." Imogene rolled her eyes. "Because it agrees perfectly with yours. If I did not know better, I would think you had coached Lady Cassandra. Besides, who is to say Lord Alanham does not possess those other qualities as well? I wonder if people sometimes think ill of those who are more popular and attractive out of jealousy."

Did some part of his dislike of Lord Alanham spring from envy? Brandon's conscience refused to grant him more latitude than it would to anyone else. On the contrary, it was far harder on him. Unable to defend himself in case he might not deserve it, he met his cousin's charge with silence.

Not so Lady Cassandra. "Surely you cannot suppose your cousin has any reason to envy Lord Alanham on point of looks, Miss Calvert. And if he does not have quite such a wide circle of friends, everyone who has the honor of acquaintance with him holds him in the highest esteem."

Her voice rang with righteous indignation that left Brandon pleasantly bemused. These hardly sounded like the sentiments of a lady for a suitor she had spurned. If he did not know better, he might suspect Cassandra Whitney held him in *more* than high esteem.

But he did know better, his sense of caution reminded him. He'd once fooled himself into believing she felt more for him than she had. It was not a mistake he intended to make again, no matter how great the temptation.

"Of course I wasn't referring to my cousin." Imogene performed a rapid turnabout. "I only meant to express my surprise that he would discourage me from thinking of his lordship in that way."

Brandon hoped Imogene would not turn the conversation back to the subject of his marriage prospects. It had provoked him to a state of near-panic earlier, when he'd feared she might mention his intentions toward Isabella Reynolds. Though he had not confided his plans to ask for the lady's hand, Imogene seemed to sense his interest went beyond casual flirtation.

But what would it matter if Lady Cassandra learned he had a new sweetheart? Brandon's heart balked at using that word in connection with Miss Reynolds. He liked the lady and considered her a safe, suitable choice for a wife. His feelings for her were not clouded by sentiment any more than hers were for him. His feelings for Lady Cassandra were quite another matter ... or could be if he did not keep them well under control. Hopefully he would not have to exercise that control long enough for it to be severely tested.

"Come now, Imogene," he said, "It is not polite for us to monopolize the conversation. What of you, Lady Cassandra, will there be a gentleman or two at Noughtly Hall who might meet your high standards and merit a little encouragement on your part?"

Perhaps if he knew she had a suitor waiting for her, it would prevent his thoughts from straying in directions they should not.

"Gentlemen at Noughtly?" Lady Cassandra shook her head. "I would be more likely to see a unicorn! But you are right to accuse me of having high standards. Far higher than I merit, no doubt. That may be why I am so firmly on the shelf."

She gave a self-deprecating chuckle. Did it carry a faint undertone of regret, Brandon wondered, or was he only hearing what he wanted to hear?

"You do not look *that* old," Imogene assured Lady Cassandra in a patronizing tone that set her cousin's teeth on edge. "I am certain there must be plenty of gentlemen who would be delighted to marry you."

Brandon bit his tongue to keep from agreeing, for fear he might sound too eager. That would never do when he was on his way to propose to another woman.

"That is kind of you, Miss Calvert." The corners of Lady Cassandra's lips arched upward in a tormented parody of a smile. "But I would far rather have no husband than the wrong one. There is nothing so capable of destroying one's happiness as a miserable marriage. I may not be able to speak from experience but …"

At that moment, Mr. Martin concluded an amusing story which drew a great swell of laughter from the other men.

It drowned out the rest of Lady Cassandra's words except to Brandon, who had leaned forward with his ears poised to catch them, "… I certainly can from observation."

Did she mean what he thought she meant? Brandon knew her late father had been married at least three times. The odds that one of those unions had been unhappy were high, if his family's experience was anything to judge by. Why had Lady Cassandra never mentioned it to him during their courtship?

For an instant he was inclined to resent her reticence. Then he recalled that he had never told her any of his family's secrets, either. During their courtship, they had formed as close an acquaintance as propriety allowed. Usually her stepmother or some other respectable chaperone hovered nearby. That was hardly conducive to soul-baring. Besides, he had wanted her to think well of him and not shy away from marrying into a family whose respectable façade concealed a shameful underside. Was it possible she had found out somehow or guessed the truth? Could that be the true reason she had refused to wed him?

Those questions plagued Brandon and made him wish he'd gotten to know her better. But there could be no opportunity for that now. For the sake of peace, they had agreed to behave like new acquaintances who knew nothing about one another.

When the other men's laughter subsided, the group on the window seat resumed their conversation. By unspoken consent, they confined themselves to impersonal subjects. Brandon's sense of caution approved, but his curiosity itched to learn more about Lady Cassandra Whitney than she had revealed to him during their decorous courtship.

Chapter Five

WHAT A STRANGE dream she'd had.

As Cassandra groped toward consciousness the next morning, she recalled the details with intense clarity. She'd been on her way to Noughtly Hall when she suddenly found herself storm-stayed with Sir Brandon Calvert.

Her imagination lingered on the sharp contours of his features and the deep, constant blue of his eye. She had dreamed of him before but always looking as he had when she'd last seen him. How had she managed to picture the way he might have matured in four years?

With a self-indulgent sigh, she tried to sink back into her dream and enjoy Sir Brandon's company for a little longer. But the waking world began to intrude. This bed did not feel like the one she shared with Vi. She was not wearing a nightgown, but the shift she wore beneath her dress during the day. Had she and Mrs. Davis reached Noughtly Hall? How strange that she could not recall it when her snowbound dream was so clear in her mind.

But if she had arrived at Noughtly, her sleeping sister should not be snuggled against her providing welcome warmth.

Cassandra's eyes flew open and her gaze ranged around the small, gabled room, still heavily cloaked in shadow. She could make out enough to realize this was neither Rosemeade Cottage nor Noughtly Hall. It must be a farmhouse on the Wiltshire Downs where she was storm-stayed with a party that included Sir Brandon Calvert!

The unmixed pleasure Cassandra had felt when she'd

believed the whole experience to be a dream suddenly became very mixed indeed. Pleasure was only a small part of that mixture — one she tried to deny altogether but could not quite.

Everything she'd seen and done the previous day came back to her. It had been one of the most distressing events she'd experienced in recent memory. Yet it had been one of the most exhilarating, too. She could congratulate herself that she had come through it with her dignity intact.

But what would today bring? Would the snow have stopped or turned to rain so she and Sir Brandon could go their separate ways?

Outside, the wind moaned around the eaves, while inside the little room, the air was filled with the drone of soft snoring from Cassandra's bedmates. Much as she dreaded subjecting herself to the chill morning air and putting on cold garments, she could not continue to lie there not knowing what today would bring. Once she knew whether she would go or stay, she could prepare herself to deal with it.

Moving as quietly as possible, so as not to wake the others, she slipped out of bed, groped about for her clothes and put them on. Shivering, she crept to the tiny window and peered through the shutter slats. Outside, the world was white as if everything had received a thick coating of meringue. Snowflakes swirled on the gusts of wind. Far from abating, they appeared to be falling harder than yesterday. So much for Sir Brandon Calvert and his confident predictions!

Cassandra barely stifled a cry of alarm when she heard a floorboard creak behind her.

"Forgive me for startling you," Mrs. Davis whispered. "How does it look out there?"

"Worse than yesterday." Cassandra shook her head. "It is a good thing Mr. and Mrs. Martin are fond of company, for I believe they will have us with them again today."

"What a blessing we found our way here." Mrs. Davis wrapped her arms around herself. Her teeth began to chatter. "If we cannot leave today, I might as well go back to bed where it is warm."

"So you should." Cassandra chafed her arms to warm them. "Now that I am up, I shall go downstairs and see if there is anything I can do. Stir up the fire and put the kettle on at least."

As Mrs. Davis started back toward the bed, Cassandra realized this might be their only opportunity for a word in private. "One more thing. Would you mind not mentioning to anyone here the reason for our visit to Aunt Augusta?"

"Of course not, my dear," Mrs. Davis gave her arm a reassuring pat. "I thought perhaps you did not wish the gentleman to know. You may rely on my discretion."

"I know I can." Grateful not to have to explain any further, Cassandra caught the woman's hand and gave it a squeeze. "Thank you. Now get back to bed before you freeze."

The poor woman was clearly relieved to oblige. She scurried back and quietly slipped beneath the covers.

Cassandra eased the bedroom door open and crept out into the narrow hallway. From one of the other rooms came the rumble of heavy snoring. Could that be Sir Brandon? Somehow she could not imagine him making such a ridiculous racket.

With bated breath and tentative footsteps, she groped her way down the winding, uneven stairs, hoping she would not wake the entire household by tumbling down. After what seemed like a very long time, she reached the parlor safely. A few stubborn embers of last night's fire cast a faint, ruddy glow over the room. Two men dozed in their chairs covered up with greatcoats. Another lay curled up on the window seat. Cassandra thought it might be Sir Brandon.

A disturbing temptation lured her to tiptoe over and watch him while he slept. She managed to resist by picturing him waking up and catching her. How humiliating that would be!

Instead she turned her steps toward the kitchen. The nearer she drew, the warmer the air seemed to grow. Cassandra thought she smelled a fire burning. Perhaps Mrs. Martin was up already, preparing to feed a houseful of unexpected guests.

"Good morning," she called softly. "What can I do to help you?"

It was not the farmwife's high-pitched voice that replied but a familiar bewitching baritone. "If you have any ability to control the weather, you might make it stop snowing. Otherwise you may refrain from criticizing my pitiful attempts to predict the future."

Sir Brandon rose from his seat at the kitchen table and greeted her with a bow.

Hard as she tried, Cassandra could not suppress a smile. She had forgotten what a comical twist Sir Brandon could put on the most commonplace remark. Perhaps she had willed herself not to recall because it would be one more thing to regret about losing him from her life.

As she approached the table, Cassandra strove to make her tone sound as carefree as his. "If I had any ability to control the weather, you may be certain I would have employed it as you suggest. I have no intention of reproaching you for hoping for the best, especially when all past experience supported your prediction."

Caution urged her to sit as far away from him possible, but she did not want them to have to speak too loudly in order to carry on a conversation. Neither did she want Sir Brandon to suppose she was afraid of him. So she sank onto the nearest chair, which happened to be beside his. "You are an early bird this morning."

"As are you." He did not sit back down at once but first fetched a cup from the sideboard. "Who would think a baronet and a duke's daughter would rise before the sun? I took the liberty of starting a fire and preparing a pot of tea. I hope the result is drinkable."

Resuming his seat, he filled the cup and slid it toward Cassandra. She raised it to her lips and took a sip. "Rather strong, but I count that in its favor. I am certain Mrs. Martin will not resent your liberties in the least, though she may be surprised to discover a baronet acting as her scullery maid. Where did you learn to make a fire and a pot of tea?"

Even before he replied, she guessed the answer. "In his Majesty's Army, of course. Military service can render a gentleman not entirely useless."

"Did you fight in many battles?" Cassandra wrapped her hands around the cup, grateful for the warmth it provided.

Sir Brandon nodded. "Talavera, Ciudad Rodrigo, Salamanca and a great many more you may never have heard of. But I will not bore you with soldiers' tales."

Cassandra doubted any such account would prove a bore. But she did shy away from hearing about any danger he had endured.

"While we have a moment alone," he continued, "I wanted to ask about something you mentioned last evening."

"What exactly?" She tried to recall their conversation.

"You told my cousin you knew the grief an unhappy marriage could cause, based upon your observation. Were you referring to your family?"

Of all the questions he might have asked her, this was the last Cassandra had expected. She chided herself for letting that private comment slip out. "Is this your idea of behaving like new acquaintances to ask such a personal question?"

Sir Brandon flinched. "I suppose not, but I should like to know just the same. Particularly if your observation of an unhappy marriage influenced your response to my proposal."

It had certainly influenced her answer to his proposal, though not in the way he might presume. Cassandra seized her cup and took a long, slow drink to keep from having to reply right away.

Sir Brandon did not push her for an answer, but neither did he try to fill the awkward silence by changing the subject, as she'd hoped he might. Instead, he sipped his tea and waited.

Perhaps she could have turned their conversation in another direction, remarking on the weather again or asking what he thought of their chances for resuming their journeys tomorrow. But part of her wanted to confide in him, in spite of the risk to her pride.

"Like many noblemen, my father was anxious to sire a male heir," she ventured at last. "If you recall your Tudor history, you may understand how that particular desire can place a strain upon a marriage."

She recalled overhearing someone jest that her father would rival Henry VIII for wives if he kept on. At the time, she'd been too young to understand what they meant. Later she understood all too well. "The strain increased with the birth of each daughter until it became desperation. My mother died giving birth to a stillborn son."

Before she knew what was happening, Sir Brandon reached out and grasped her hand. "I beg your pardon. I should not have asked a question that was bound to prompt painful memories."

His touch brought back some of the most pleasant memories of her life. Memories of stolen moments when her chaperone's attention was diverted and Sir Brandon took advantage of it to clasp her hand. How much that brief, chaste contact between them had communicated — admiration, affection and a desire to protect her. If her touch had conveyed her true feelings to him, no wonder her rejection had puzzled him. Had it driven him to seek a reason that made more sense than the one she'd given him?

His present touch communicated different feelings, but ones Cassandra valued no less — regret, compassion and a wish to provide comfort.

Yet she was receiving all this bounty from his generous heart under false pretenses. "I have no memories of my mother, painful or otherwise. I was too young when she died. However, I am informed my sister Viola is very like her."

To her surprise, Sir Brandon did not release her hand, but tightened his grasp. "I believe it might be worse to have no recollection at all."

Cassandra shook her head. "I assure you it is not. I recall

my father's second wife very well — Miranda and Evelina's mother. She was as devoted to Viola and me as our own mama could have been if she'd lived. Losing her was very hard indeed, but no worse than knowing how unhappy Father made her because she bore him only daughters."

More than half her life she had locked that knowledge and those emotions away in her heart. She had concealed them even from Vi, who had loved their father and been loved as she and the others had never been. Though it affronted her pride to betray such vulnerability, it brought Cassandra an unexpected sense of relief to unburden herself.

"Poor Letty had it worst of all," she continued, forced by some bewildering compulsion to confess fully once she had begun, "because she bore him no children at all. Much as she regretted it, that misfortune probably saved her life."

There was more she could reveal, but it was far more humiliating and she had vowed never to speak of it.

"Forgive me. I do not know what to say." Sir Brandon's gaze, more compassionate than she had ever beheld it, seemed to caress her face and her very heart.

If she allowed him to continue, Cassandra feared she would be lost. "Perhaps that is because you have no experience of such bitterness within a family."

By a resolute act of will, she pried her hand from his strong, comforting grasp. "After all, your father had two sons to safeguard his family title."

Sir Brandon flinched as if she had struck him. A cold wave of remorse washed over her, though Cassandra did not understand its cause.

His features and his eyes betrayed an inner struggle of a kind she knew all too well. A struggle between the irresistible compulsion to speak and the immoveable safeguards put in place to prevent it.

"Believe me . . ." The words burst out of him. ". . . that provided no guarantee of family harmony!"

Cassandra suspected once the stout wall of silence had

been breeched, further confidences would follow, as they had with her. But before Sir Brandon could say more, the sound of approaching footsteps sealed his lips.

"Well, well, what's this?" Mrs. Martin bustled in. "To think I should lie abed while a lady and gentleman were up lighting the fire. Good morning my dears. Why did you not strike a light? We can afford candles, you know."

Sir Brandon quickly recovered his composure and began to chat with their hostess most amiably. It took Cassandra longer to recover hers. A dozen questions clamored in her mind that she longed to put to him. But would she find another private moment before the storm abated and they were obliged to part company again?

Brandon welcomed the sudden appearance of Mrs. Martin as he once had greeted the arrival of reinforcing troops to lift a desperate siege. He could scarcely bear to contemplate what he might have revealed to Lady Cassandra, if not for the timely intervention of their hostess.

And yet, part of him resented the intrusion on a precious moment of mutual confidence between them. Never during the weeks of their courtship, had he suspected the bruised spirit hidden behind Cassandra Whitney's gallant smiles and challenging banter. He had envied her seemingly devoted family. Clearly the affection among the sisters and their stepmother had been sincere. But he'd also believed her father was proud of Cassandra and that she had been eager to please him. Now Brandon knew better.

Mrs. Martin lit a candle from the fire and placed it on the table. Then she took a seat opposite Brandon and Lady Cassandra. "It looks as if you will be staying with us another day at least. I fear your poor cousin will not be pleased to miss more of that fine house party."

"Don't mind Imogene, I beg you." Brandon rose and fetched a cup for Mrs. Martin, who beamed at him with more approval than he had ever received from his own celebrated mother. "She is young and not as sensible as she might be. To be quite truthful, I find *this* house party more congenial than I expect to find the one at Everleigh."

Mrs. Martin chuckled as she poured herself tea. "I reckon you find the *company* here more to your liking."

She cast a significant glance toward Lady Cassandra.

Were his feelings that obvious? Brandon fought down a rising wave of alarm. How could that be when he did not know his own feelings? Did he not know them, his conscience demanded, or could he not bring himself to admit what they might be?

Nonsense! There was nothing to admit. Surely it would take more than twelve hours and two conversations to rekindle any feelings for Lady Cassandra after four years of determined effort to quench them.

"I believe you may be correct, Mrs. Martin," he replied because he had to say something. "I fear some of the company at Everleigh may prove quite tiresome."

It was true. Apart from the Norrington's nephew, Lord Sandiford, Miss Reynolds and her brother, he expected the Everleigh party to include a number of drawling young bucks and several vapid debutantes who would make his cousin sound like a bluestocking by comparison.

Fortunately their hostess did not question his remark but turned her attention to Lady Cassandra. "You look very well this morning, my dear. Being storm-stayed must agree with you."

Lady Cassandra gave a weak chuckle and raised her hand to her hair, which had been loosely plaited for the night and remained so. Several dark tendrils had worked free to curl around her face. "Your eyes must be playing tricks on you Mrs. Martin. Or perhaps this candlelight is more than usually forgiving. I should be afraid to look in a mirror!"

She had nothing to fear from such an inspection. Brandon bit his tongue to keep from voicing that thought. But he could not prevent his gaze from lingering upon her.

There was nothing wrong with Mrs. Martin's vision. Nor could the candlelight take all the credit for Cassandra's winsome appearance. It did bring out the warm chestnut highlights in her dark hair and lent her complexion a rosy glow that made her look younger than her years. But was it also responsible for the sparkle in her deep brown eyes and the becoming air of softness about her features?

His hand still tingled from its recent contact with hers. But now it began to ache with the urge to cup her chin or trail the back of his fingers over her cheek. He clutched the handle of his cup tight to keep such dangerous impulses in check.

Meanwhile their hostess continued to smile at them as if she knew some amusing secret of which they were unaware. If he had not been so grateful to her and her husband, Brandon might have found her behavior rather vexing.

"You must tell us what we can do to assist you today." Lady Cassandra changed the subject, much to Brandon's relief. "It is no easy task to look after a houseful of people at the best of times."

Brandon nodded. "There are chores that must be done no matter what the weather."

His years in the army had taught him that. But where had a duke's daughter learned how much effort was required to tend so many guests?

Their hostess considered for a moment. Her broad smile faded a little and her brow furrowed. "I will need a path made to the well and water fetched. The stock will need feeding and mucking out and the cows must be milked even if it was raining fire and brimstone. I reckon the eggs will need to be gathered. Then there's always the fires to be tended and the cooking ... and the washing up, of course."

"I can help with those at least and fetching the eggs," Cassandra volunteered.

"I will beat a path to your well and draw water," Brandon offered, not to be outdone. "I am certain the others will be anxious to help out in any way they can."

With the exception of Imogene. Brandon could not picture his cousin turning her hand to household tasks. He feared what a mess she might make of them if she tried.

All too soon the rest of the company began to wake and wander out to the kitchen. Brandon knew he ought to be grateful for the buffer their presence created between him and Cassandra. After all, he did not want to risk revealing more about his family or face whatever questions his earlier comments might provoke from her. Yet when he recalled those moments of murmured confidences in the shadowy farmhouse kitchen, he yearned to bundle everyone else out into the snow so he might have Cassandra all to himself again.

He should not think such things! Brandon tried to blame his wayward inclinations on a lack of sleep. Nothing must stand in the way of his plan to marry Miss Reynolds — especially not a hopeless infatuation with a woman who had made her unwillingness to wed him quite clear.

His effort to forget the past and treat her like a newly-met acquaintance had failed. His hopes for the storm to subside had come to nothing. Trying to ignore her had proven impossible as long as he could see or hear her. Clearly he needed to put some distance between them by any means necessary.

With that aim in mind, he bundled up and ventured outside to make a path to the well. He threw himself into the task, dragging a large square board weighted with rocks until his hands blistered and his arms threatened to wrench out of their sockets. Yet he quickly discovered that repetitive manual labor left his mind free to wander wherever it chose. That was inevitably in the direction of Lady Cassandra Whitney. The unrelieved whiteness of his surroundings and the air full of wafting snowflakes provided no distraction when he most needed one. He must find a more challenging activity to occupy his thoughts!

The cold finally drove him back inside where Mrs. Martin was effusive in her thanks. "It's a blessing that well is good and deep. I was half afraid you might find the water frozen.

Now come sit by the fire and thaw yourself out."

"Has the snow eased at all?" asked Imogene, who was seated at the table eating bread and butter.

His cousin's hair was pinned in a simple but pretty style, as was Lady Cassandra's. Brandon noted the latter with a faint qualm of regret. He preferred the loose braid she'd worn earlier. He wished he could once see her rich, dark hair entirely unbound.

Blast! He was not supposed to think such things. He was not supposed to look at her.

"Far from it," he answered his cousin's question. Frustration with himself and their situation sharpened his words. "The snow is coming down harder than ever. Heaven knows when the roads will be fit to travel."

"What about our luggage?" Imogene wailed.

"What about it?" Brandon sank onto a chair in the corner nook beside the kitchen hearth. "We did not bring a great deal with us and what we did is stowed in the boot of the stagecoach."

"What if someone steals it?" his cousin demanded. "I heard the farmer and the coach-driver talking about highwaymen who rob coaches on this road."

Mrs. Martin laughed as she cooled steaming water from the kettle with some Brandon had fetched from the well. "That was thirty years ago, Miss. Even if they'd still been around, the Cherhill Gang would never have disturbed your carriage."

"Why not?" Somehow Imogene sounded disappointed that their luggage might be safe from theft.

"Because, that lot only worked in warm weather." Mrs. Martin grated a bit of soap into the washbasin. "They used to rob coaches stark naked. It shocked folks so bad they did not put up a fight and afterwards no one could give a proper description of the thieves."

Brandon could not contain a hoot of laughter at such comical audacity, but Imogene looked thoroughly shocked by the notion of naked highwaymen. Lady Cassandra tried to stifle a grin, but did not succeed.

Too late Brandon remembered he was not supposed to be looking at her. His eyes seemed to have developed a will of their own.

"But I cannot wear the same dress day after day," Imogene protested. "I need proper nightclothes and my own comb. Can't someone go and fetch them?"

Brandon could think of a dozen reasons why such an expedition should be out of the question. But it would take him away from Lady Cassandra and provide him with a task difficult and dangerous enough to keep his thoughts from straying in undesirable directions.

Not undesirable, he reflected as he watched her drying dishes for Mrs. Martin. If anything, far *too* desirable. "Once I have warmed up a little, I will see what I can do."

Imogene clapped her hands but Lady Cassandra cried, "No, you must not! Remember what it was like last night? It has snowed a great deal more since then."

Did she think he was not capable of the task? He would show her. "That was different. The light was fading. We had no idea where we were going or how long it would take to get there,"

"What if you lose your way?" she challenged him. "I would wear the same dress for a year rather than risk your safety!"

She was worried about him? Brandon's heart bounded. That did not mean she cared for him in any particular way, reason insisted. She might have said the same about the coach guard or his footman.

"That is kind of you," he replied. "But I do not expect to be in any danger. It will be light for hours yet and we can retrace our steps through the snow on our return journey."

"Of course you can!" Imogene sprang from her seat and flew to offer Brandon a grateful embrace.

He glanced up to find Lady Cassandra watching them. In spite of her fierce scowl, the slant of her brows somehow suggested that she wished she could change places with his cousin.

Or was he only imagining it because that was what *he* wished? All the more reason why he needed to escape the confines of this house and his bedeviling proximity to the woman he'd once hoped to make his wife.

Chapter Six

"PLEASE RECONSIDER THIS foolhardy idea," Cassandra implored Sir Brandon as he, his footman and the coach guard donned their greatcoats, hats and mufflers. "We can manage well enough with what we have for another day or two. Surely by then the weather will have improved."

How could his cousin have been so selfish as to urge him into danger for the sake of her girlish vanity?

"I do not consider the scheme foolhardy." He refused to meet her gaze but concentrated on fastening the buttons of his coat. "We will all be a good deal more comfortable with a change of linen. The stagecoach cannot be farther than two miles."

"That is near enough in ordinary weather," she agreed. "But in such deep snow a hundred yards can be a vast distance to travel. Do not forget, you will have to go there *and* back, dragging heavy trunks on the return journey."

She studied his features with almost jealous intensity seeking any sign of second thoughts she might exploit. Instead her warning seemed to have the opposite affect, rousing Sir Brandon's stubbornness.

"When did you become such a worrywart?" he demanded. "The Cassandra Whitney I recall used to be quite intrepid."

It was clear he disapproved of the ways she had changed during the past four years. That hurt more than she cared to admit. The hurt struck against her fear for him, igniting her temper. "I grew up! I learned that my actions have consequences and that I must consider them before I jump in with both feet."

"Are you saying I am heedless as well as foolhardy?" His tone sharpened to match hers.

"You are certainly not heeding *me*." Her stomach churned and her eyes prickled ominously. They threatened a mortifying burst of tears if she did not soon get her emotions under control.

Before Sir Brandon could reply, his footman interrupted their argument. "Begging your pardon, sir. The two of us can go fetch the luggage if you need to stay behind."

Cassandra could have kissed the young man. Then she reminded herself it was too risky an errand for *anyone*. She should be concerned for all of them — not only Sir Brandon.

"Nonsense!" he snapped. "I would never order anyone to do what I would not do myself. We are going to do this, all three of us, and that is final."

He made a curt bow that was dismissive rather than respectful. "Pray excuse us, Lady Cassandra. The sooner we go, the sooner we shall return and the more light we will have to find our way."

There was no lack of light outside. Cassandra had found the glaring whiteness almost blinding when she'd waded out to the barn to collect eggs for Mrs. Martin. That would not make it easier for Brandon and the others to find their way.

The door opened and the other two men trudged outside. Sir Brandon turned away from her to follow them.

Cassandra lunged toward him and grasped the sleeve of his coat, tugging with all her might. "Please Bran — I cannot let you do this!"

Had she addressed him in such a familiar way? The intensity of feeling her actions betrayed shocked Cassandra. But if it kept him from harm, surely it would be worthwhile.

But her final desperate plea availed no more than the others. Instead of hesitating, Brandon swung his arm with fierce strength, wrenching his sleeve from her grasp. His blue eyes blazed with the frosty intensity of a blizzard that raged inside him. "Enough, Cassandra! Do not pretend you care what happens to me!"

She staggered back as if he had driven a jagged shard of ice deep into her heart. *Pretend to care?* No indeed. She had spent years pretending to the world, and most of all to herself, that she *did not* care anything about the suitor she'd spurned. In truth she did care, far more than she could afford to, about what had happened to him in the past and what would happen in the future.

Now all she could do was to watch helplessly as he strode out into the storm and slammed the door behind him.

Should he have swallowed his pride and heeded Cassandra?

As Brandon waded through the snow straining to spot the stagecoach and maintain his bearings, he began to think it might have been the more prudent course. But he found it impossible to behave prudently where she was concerned, as he had almost from the moment they met.

It had not been prudent for a mere baronet to aspire to the daughter of a future duke. Yet once they were introduced, he could not rest until he'd made an effort to win her. He hoped today's rash decision would end better than that.

Dash it all! He was doing it again — mooning over Lady Cassandra when he most needed to keep his wits about him. Even the faint sting of snowflakes the winter wind whipped against his face could not chase the lady from his thoughts for long.

"I have never seen so much snow at one time," his footman, shouted to be heard over the wail of the wind. "Everything is just white mounds. How will we tell the stagecoach from anything else?"

"It will be a very tall mound, Edward!" Brandon called back, ending with a loud laugh that he hoped would ease the young man's obvious anxiety.

He was doing enough worrying for all three of them. Not that they would become lost, for there was still a shallow trough visible in the snow that marked the way they had come yesterday. As long as they followed that, it would lead them to the coach. Coming back, the path would be clearer still, as he had tried to reassure Cassandra.

What he had not reckoned on was the effort it took to wallow through the snow that had drifted waist-deep in places. Though he believed himself to be in reasonable condition after all the riding and marching he had done in Spain, the exertion was beginning to take its toll on him. The muscles in his legs and torso cramped from the strain. His heart pounded hard against his ribs. When he gasped in the raw winter air, it seemed to slash through his lungs. Edward and the coach guard were in no better shape. What if there came a moment when they could not stagger another step?

He would not let that happen! Brandon insisted, as if he were addressing Lady Cassandra rather than himself. He would do whatever he must to prevent any harm coming to the others.

Pausing for a moment to catch his breath, he turned toward Edward and the coach guard, who was leading the largest and strongest of the horses.

"I am certain we have walked nearly as far as we did last night." He angled his back to take the brunt of the north wind, which roared down from the high ground. "If we do not spot the coach very soon, we must turn back."

He could picture the fuss his cousin would make if they returned empty-handed, not to mention Lady Cassandra gloating over being proved right. Or would she? He had accused her of only pretending to care what became of him. What if he'd been wrong and her concern was genuine?

The other men nodded vigorously. Even the horse tossed its head as if in agreement.

"The wind is blowing harder than ever," the coach guard shouted. "If it drifts in our tracks, we may have a devil of a time finding our way back."

The man's words chilled Brandon like a bit of melting

snow trickling down his back. If the worst befell him before he'd had an opportunity to sire an heir, his mother's betrayal would be rewarded. He could not let that happen.

If any harm befell Brandon, part of the responsibility would be on her head.

That thought haunted Cassandra throughout the afternoon. She threw herself into every household chore she could badger Mrs. Martin into finding for her. The time still crawled along like cold treacle.

Seated in a chair near the parlor fire, Imogene Calvert sipped her tea and fretted. "What is taking them so long? I thought they would be back by now."

Cassandra fought the urge to fly across the room and shake the selfish little ninny until her teeth rattled. "I tried to tell your cousin it would not be as easy an errand as you and he expected. I wish he had listened to me."

Miss Calvert smirked. "If you did not want him to go, you shouldn't have opposed him so strenuously. I do believe your warnings only spurred Brandon's determination to go."

Cassandra pressed her lips together to stifle a cowardly whimper. Imogene Calvert's words confirmed her own worst fears. She should have remembered that opposition always strengthened Sir Brandon's resolve. She should have moderated her response accordingly, giving him an opportunity to reconsider the idea on his own. Instead she had driven him out into the storm. In the process, she had destroyed the fragile truce between them that might have ripened into something even more cordial.

She did not dare answer his cousin for fear of what she might say. Instead she glanced at the Martins' mantel clock to discover how little time had passed since she'd last looked. Was there something wrong with the timepiece? Perhaps it needed winding.

She hurried to the kitchen to ask Mrs. Martin, who shook her head. "Tobias winds that clock every night before bed and yesterday was no exception. The time only passes slowly for you because you're fretting over the gentleman."

Cassandra opened her mouth to deny it but a shrewd look from the older woman warned her not to waste her breath.

"Sit down, have a cup of tea and calm yourself," Mrs. Martin ordered in a tone that sounded brisk, but not without sympathy. "I reckon the men will be back before long with no worse harm than a chill. They're young and fit and Sir Brandon seems a great deal more capable than most gentlemen."

The instant the words were out of her mouth, she raised her fingers to her lips as if she wished to stuff them back in. "Begging your pardon, my lady! You've been such a help to me, I forgot myself."

"No offense taken." Cassandra assured her, dropping onto a seat at the kitchen table. "I am acquainted with enough noblemen to know you are not wrong in your judgment. It is not Sir Brandon's ability I question, only the severity of the conditions he faces."

She accepted a steaming cup of tea with a murmur of thanks, hoping that conversation with Mrs. Martin would prove a more effective distraction from her worries then her household chores had. She recalled how swiftly time had flown that morning when she and Brandon had talked and sipped tea in the darkened kitchen. Cassandra only wished she could have made it last longer.

Mrs. Martin poured herself a cup of tea and sat down opposite Cassandra. "Whatever happened between you in the past, you're still very partial to him, aren't you?"

Cassandra considered denying her feelings but sensed she would not be believed. She gave a brief nod only to discover how pleasant it felt to admit her long-concealed emotions.

"I tried to stop for the sake of my peace of mind." She sighed. "I persuaded myself I had. When I saw him again, it all came flooding back and I cannot seem to control it."

"Then don't." Mrs. Martin's motherly sympathy was balm to Cassandra's turbulent heart. "No good ever comes of trying to make yourself feel contrary to what your heart decides. What happened between the two of you, anyhow? Are you certain matters cannot be mended now that some time has passed?"

"Quite certain!" Cassandra's hand trembled as she raised her cup, spattering hot drops of tea over the rustic tabletop. She could not afford to hope such a thing might be possible. "I insulted and injured him in a manner I cannot expect him to forgive."

"Were you untrue?" Mrs. Martin sounded reluctant to pose such a personal question. Yet Cassandra knew she was asking out of more than idle curiosity.

"Of course not!" Her denial rose instinctively. Yet once the words were out, her conscience grew uneasy.

Certainly she had not done what Mrs. Martin meant. She had never encouraged another gentleman during her courtship with Brandon — or since for that matter. She had been true *to* him but she had not been altogether truthful *with* him.

Mrs. Martin's pale ginger brows lowered in a look of puzzlement. "Then what on earth could you have done that would be so difficult to forgive?"

Long habit tried to seal Cassandra's lips on the subject. But her recent confessions to Brandon and their hostess had weakened her resolve to keep silent. Besides she needed to impress upon Mrs. Martin the futility of hoping for any sort of reconciliation with her former suitor. Otherwise, she feared their hostess might not be above a little innocent matchmaking.

"I . . . rejected his proposal." She hung her head knowing Mrs. Martin would think ill of her once she knew. "I refused after giving every indication that I cared for him and would be honored to accept."

"But why would you do such a thing, my dear?" Mrs. Martin did not sound reproachful, only bewildered and disappointed.

That secret would require a great deal more effort to confess, though Cassandra sensed the stout wards upon it were beginning to weaken. "I had my reasons and I still believe they were sound ones. If we had wed, I feel certain our marriage would have been most unhappy. He would have come to despise me even more than he does now. At least this way I have the satisfaction of knowing I did the honorable thing ... even if he believes otherwise."

Mrs. Martin reached across the table and patted her hand. "You believed you were doing what was best for him?"

Cassandra raised her head and answered in a tone of perfect assurance. "I am certain of it."

"It could not have been easy, though, could it?" Mrs. Martin sounded regretful ... even pitying. Yet an undertone of admiration made that pity bearable, the way a dose of sweet syrup made it possible to swallow foul-tasting medicine. "It must have cost you a good bit of heartache at the time and ever since."

Cassandra nodded. "It was a price I was willing to pay and I would again."

"I think you ought to tell Sir Brandon everything you've told me." Mrs. Martin gave a resolute nod and refilled both their cups. "The poor man must assume you were trifling with his affections. He may have thought you didn't care for him because he wasn't worth caring for."

The thought appalled Cassandra. "Surely he cannot believe that!"

He was the finest man she'd ever met. It had never crossed her mind that he could possibly think otherwise.

Mrs. Martin gave a doubtful shrug. "Folk often don't regard themselves as highly as others do. Why do you suppose he's never found a wife since then?"

Had her rejection affected him that badly? Cassandra did not want to believe it. "He served in Spain with General Wellington's army and only returned a few months ago."

That perfectly reasonable explanation did not satisfy her sympathetic inquisitor. "Why do you reckon he joined the army in the first place?"

"That had nothing to do with me!" It could not have ...

could it? The possibility distressed Cassandra in spite of her vigorous denial.

"I wouldn't be too sure," Mrs. Martin shook her head. "At least not until you ask him outright."

Cassandra scrambled up from the table. Her face felt as if it were on fire. "I have no intention of asking him any such thing! That is all water under the bridge. No good can come of stirring it all up again."

But what if Mrs. Martin was right? What if she had driven Brandon to the perils of the battlefield just as she had driven him out into the storm today? In her desperation to protect him, had she only forced him into greater peril?

"I do not mean to tell him about *anything* we have discussed just now," she repeated for emphasis, "I must insist you treat it as a confidence and say nothing to Sir Brandon, either."

"Very well, my dear, if that is what you wish." The tone of Mrs. Martin's agreement told Cassandra she would like to meddle if permitted. "I promise I will not breathe a word to the gentleman about what you have told me."

"It *is* what I wish," Cassandra confirmed, so there could be no possible doubt.

She chided herself for fretting so much about what Mrs. Martin might say to Brandon when she should be more concerned about his safe return.

"What can be taking them so long?" She echoed his cousin's question, but in a tone of anxiety rather than annoyance. "They should have been back before this, even if the going was difficult."

It haunted her to think of Brandon out there in the cold, unable to find his way, with every step a struggle. If any harm befell him out there, how would she bear it? She would have to grieve in secret, for no one would understand her feelings. She would have no claim on the sympathy due a grieving widow or even a bereaved sweetheart.

Then she heard the Martins' dog bark. It had been a welcome sound last night, but was a hundred times more to

Cassandra at that moment.

Just … one … more … step. Brandon urged his exhausted body and frostbitten extremities with a litany that was half exhortation and half promise. His body had long since ceased to believe the promise.

"Are we still going the right way, sir?" Edward called. He clung to the horse's girth on the right-hand side while the coach guard held onto the left. Brandon led the creature by the bridle, his eyes fixed forward.

The wind had blown snow into their tracks, making the trail harder and harder to follow. The only saving grace was that it gusted down from the north, leaving a slight hollow on one side. It was not always easy to spot, but it was better than nothing.

"We are!" he shouted back, trying to infuse his voice with optimism. "It cannot be much farther."

That was what kept him staggering forward — the dogged determination to get the others back safely … and the prospect of seeing Cassandra again. At first he had tried to dismiss that thought. But as step followed labored step and other inducements failed, the image of her continued to draw him on.

"Do you hear that?" The coach guard cried. "I think it's the Martins' dog."

Brandon could not hear anything over the shriek of the wind. That did not stop him from crying, "You see? I told you it could not be far!"

He feared the effect on their spirits if it turned out to be wrong. But after a few more steps, he could hear the dog quite clearly.

Then Podger came bounding toward them, followed by Mr. Martin, the coachman and Brandon's driver.

"Back at last!" called the farmer. "We were beginning to think you might have kept on going all the way to Marlborough."

The coachman took Brandon's place leading the horse and they all trudged back to the barn.

"Get into the house and thaw out," Mr. Martin ordered Brandon and his companions. "We'll unload this lot. The trunks can stay here in the barn. They'll be dry and folks can fetch what they need."

Brandon was too tired to do more than nod. He lurched toward the house, grateful beyond measure to whoever had made a path to the door.

As he pushed it open, a wave of warm air billowed over him, fragrant with the aroma of new bread, roast meat and spiced apples. Even better than those mouth-watering smells was the sight of Cassandra, flushed and smiling with a suspicious glint of moisture in her dark eyes.

For an instant Brandon thought she might throw her arms around him. His heart leapt at the prospect. But she only seized his arm and drew him deeper into the entry hall to make room for the men behind him.

He could not be too disappointed, however. For when she spoke, the relief in her voice seemed to embrace him. "Come in, come in! You must be frozen. We were growing quite worried about you.

She took his hat and brushed the snow from it, then helped him out of his greatcoat with brisk but attentive movements.

Imogene hovered behind her. "Did you bring the luggage?"

Brandon replied with a weary nod. "We would not have dared come back without it."

"You returned safe and sound," said Cassandra as she hung up his coat. "That is all that matters."

She was not *pretending* to care about his safe return. Brandon's intuition assured him without the slightest qualm of doubt. Perhaps when he recovered his strength, he could persuade himself otherwise. For the moment he was more than content to bask in the delightful warmth of her welcome.

Chapter Seven

HARD AS SHE tried to keep the perilous surge of happiness from overwhelming her, Cassandra found it impossible.

Brandon had returned safe. Just then, nothing else mattered. Her regrets about the past dwindled into insignificance. So did her fear that he might discover the truth about her feelings or her circumstances. What a relief it was to have their weight lifted from her heart, buoyed by a rising tide of uncomplicated joy.

She pulled a chair close to the parlor fire and gave him a gentle push onto it. As she pried off his boots and chafed his icy feet, she soaked up every instant of contact between them. Mrs. Martin and Mrs. Davis tended to the other men with motherly solicitude for which Cassandra was thankful. Otherwise her actions might have betrayed her feelings to everyone present … not that it would have stopped her.

"You will need something stronger than tea to warm you," Mrs. Martin declared. "More mulled cider should do the trick."

Cassandra flew to the kitchen and fetched a tall mug of cider for Brandon. Then she hovered nearby as he drank.

After a few moments, he looked up at her with a wry grin that made her insides quiver. "You are showing remarkable restraint, Lady Cassandra."

"I … I am?" Was he mocking her? The way she'd fussed over him had not been *restrained* in the least. "In what way?"

His blue eyes twinkled. "By refraining from reminding me that you warned against venturing out in the storm. You were right. It was not worth the risk of three lives … four if you count the horse."

Cassandra shook her head. "You will hear no reproaches from me. I should have held my tongue. Then you might have reconsidered the idea for yourself rather than becoming all the more determined to go."

"Are you trying to say it is *your* fault I am a stubborn ass?"

"Yes ... I mean ... no!" she stammered while the others laughed. "That is ... I should have borne in mind your headstrong nature when I tried to dissuade you."

"You did what you could to prevent us from going." All the levity disappeared from his gaze, replaced by sincere gratitude that absolved her self-blame. "I should have thanked you for your concern instead of scoffing at your warnings."

It was a good thing he had absolved her of responsibility, because the other two men began to talk about their ordeal. They spoke of icy wind that cut through many layers of clothing, and deep, shifting snow that was like wading through quicksand. Swirling, fast-falling flakes had made it impossible to see more than a few feet in any direction. Though they were safe now, it sickened Cassandra to think how easily they might have been lost.

It made her want to cling to Brandon, though she knew she had no right, to satisfy herself that he was safe and well. Deeply ingrained propriety kept her from hurling herself into his arms, but she could not prevent her gaze from lingering upon him and her ears from straining to catch the sound of his voice.

To her disappointment, he did not have much to add to the other men's account. Now that the danger had passed, they seemed eager to recount every harrowing detail. Did it remind him of the danger they'd faced, magnifying *his* sense of responsibility?

After a time, Mr. Martin and the other men came in from the barn. Cassandra and Mrs. Davis withdrew to the kitchen to help Mrs. Martin get dinner on the table. Miss Calvert remained behind in the parlor, begging their host to have her small trunk of *absolute necessities* brought into the house. By the time everyone crowded around the kitchen table for a meal of hearty stew, the lady had won his reluctant consent.

"I suppose there might be room for the ladies' luggage," said Mr. Martin, clearly not wishing to favor Miss Calvert over the others.

Cassandra shook her head. "Mine can stay in the barn. Whatever I need, I can fetch from there. The fresh air will do me good."

Miss Calvert wrinkled up her nose. "Aren't you worried your clothes will smell of the barn?"

The others laughed but Brandon cast his cousin a reproachful look.

"There are far worse smells they could pick up," Cassandra replied, anxious to lessen any insult to their hosts. "My father used to smoke and the odor from it clung to everything in the house."

Conversation soon returned to the expedition to fetch their luggage. The older men were anxious to hear the story and Sir Brandon's companions seemed pleased to be the center of attention. Cassandra half-wished he would join in their tale so she could hear his voice and have an excuse to look at him with more than furtive glances.

"It was the most miserable weather I have ever been out in," concluded the young footman. "What about you, Sir Brandon?"

The question seemed to catch the baronet off-guard. He gave a mild start, as if roused from thoughts that preoccupied him. Then, to Cassandra's surprise, he shook his head. "This afternoon was a pleasant winter frolic compared to the British retreat from Tordesillas last year."

As soon as Sir Brandon spoke, he seemed to regret it. He seized his cider mug and took a long drink, perhaps to keep from saying more. But it was too late.

Mr. Martin perked up at the mention of the battle. "Were you in Spain with General Wellington?"

Brandon gave a grim nod. "I was there from shortly before the Battle of Talavera until Vitoria last spring. It has been a hard campaign, but Bonaparte's troops are on the run at last. I should not be surprised if the war is successfully concluded in a few months' time."

"Tell us about that *Tortoise* place," urged the stagecoach guard. "Did it snow there as well?"

The man sounded eager to hear more, as if he envied the baronet's participation in some great adventure. Cassandra's reaction was quite the opposite. She could not forget Mrs. Martin's suggestion that Brandon might have enlisted in the army because she'd rejected his offer of marriage.

"We might have been better off if it *had* snowed." The baronet replied with an air of reluctance. "Then the roads might have frozen into a firm surface we could have walked on instead of slogging through clay mud thick enough to suck a man's boots off. The rain was nearly as cold as snow. It soaked us to the skin, making the wind chill us all the worse."

Even in the snug, dry kitchen with a roaring fire at his back, the memory made Brandon shiver. He glanced down at his empty plate. "I would have paid a king's ransom for a bit of bread on that cursed march. The quartermaster sent our supplies by the wrong road, so we lived on roasted acorns and a pig we caught foraging. We lost as many men from cold and hunger on that retreat as we might have fighting a battle, with nothing to show for it in the end."

As he spoke, vivid, accusing images flooded Cassandra's mind. Brandon had assured her she was not responsible for sending him out into discomfort and danger today. But what about four years ago? Whatever she'd meant to spare him by rejecting his proposal, it could not have been worse than what he'd suffered during his military service on the Peninsula.

Brandon glanced toward her then with a look that seemed to hold her accountable for what he'd endured. Or was it only her own conscience accusing her?

"One of the lads from the village was lost in the war about

that time," Mr. Martin mused. "I thought he must have been killed in battle. Now I wonder if he perished on that retreat, poor fellow."

"Well, there will be no starving here tonight." Mrs. Martin did not sound as if she approved of the somber turn the conversation had taken. "I've made a lovely pudding and I hope you've all saved room for it."

"Oh, aye." "Yes indeed." The others replied in various ways that signaled their eagerness.

Were they only grateful for Mrs. Martin's toothsome pudding, or for an opportunity to lift the mood around the table as well?

Cassandra welcomed the excuse to rise from her place and help Mrs. Martin serve out hearty slabs of the dense, raisin-studded pudding. When she slid a piece onto Brandon's plate, he murmured his thanks and cast her a look she could not properly interpret.

The rest of the party began to discuss the hopeful turn the war had taken during the past year. Brandon did not join in, though he must be the most knowledgeable on the subject. Instead he seemed to sink back into his thoughts.

Had the events of the afternoon and the recent conversation roused disturbing memories of his experiences during the War? Were those the stories with which he had not wanted to *bore* her when they'd spoken together that morning? Perhaps it would have been more apt to say he had not wanted to *horrify* her.

What had provoked him to bring up that miserable business of the retreat from Tordesillas? Brandon chided himself as the party retired to the parlor after dinner. The wretched details were hardly the stuff of polite mealtime conversation. The pallor that had come over Cassandra's face as he spoke, and the stricken look in her dark eyes, had reproached him for his lack of consideration.

But when the coach guard had inquired about the retreat

in a tone that suggested war was some kind of romantic adventure, Brandon could not permit such a popular misconception to go unchallenged. He was sorry to have distressed Cassandra, though, particularly after the worry he'd caused her earlier.

Yesterday he would not have believed Lady Cassandra Whitney capable of caring about the fate of nameless soldiers who had lost their lives on that terrible march. Now, he began to suspect her experiences during the past four years had changed Cassandra, as his had changed him. That did not make her any less dangerous to his hard-won peace of mind, yet the thought still soothed him somehow. It made him want to talk to her again, the way they had that morning, even if it meant she might ask questions he did not wish to answer.

She and Mrs. Davis had stayed behind in the kitchen to help Mrs. Martin clear the table and wash the dishes. The other two women now rejoined the party in the parlor, but there was no sign of Cassandra.

"Can I fetch you a drop more cider, Sir Brandon?" Mrs. Martin inquired.

"You have done more than enough to see to my comfort for one day, ma'am," he replied. "You should take a seat and enjoy a few minutes of well-deserved leisure. If it would not be imposing upon your hospitality, I will help myself to a bit more of your excellent cider, along with anyone else who would care to have their cup refilled."

He thought Mrs. Martin might insist on doing the honors, but instead she sank onto an empty chair and lavished him with a grateful smile. "You would not be imposing in the least, sir. While you and the others are our guests, we would like you to make yourselves quite at home. I would not refuse a drink while you are fetching more for yourself."

Brandon asked the others but no one else seemed thirsty at the moment. So he strode off to the kitchen with the assurance of having a good excuse to take him there. He thought back to the previous night when he had surprised Cassandra alone in the kitchen and suggested they treat one another like new acquaintances. His attitude had altered so much since then that he found it hard to believe only twenty-four hours had passed.

After his recent trek through the snow, he had serious doubts they would be going their separate ways any time soon. Trying to forget their past connection was not a workable solution if they were to remain snowbound together for much longer. A more sensible course might be to face their past with the benefit of hindsight and greater maturity. Perhaps if they could talk over what had happened between them, and acknowledge its effects on their hearts and their lives, they could truly put it behind them once and for all.

He ignored a tempting whisper in the back of his mind that questioned whether an older and wiser Lady Cassandra might regard him more favorably than the headstrong debutante of four years ago. He had learned his lesson. Once bitten, twice shy, as the saying went. Her rejection had dealt his heart a wound that had taken longer than expected to heal. He could not afford to risk another.

He entered the kitchen, expecting to find Cassandra bustling about to keep herself occupied. Instead he discovered her sitting at the table with her face buried in her folded arms. For an instant he wondered if she'd fallen asleep. After all, she had risen very early that morning.

Then her shoulders heaved and a silent shudder ran through her willowy frame. The sight of her weeping demolished all Brandon's sensible intentions. A pair of powerful, invisible hands seemed to tighten around his throat. The only way to break their hold was to do anything in his power to relieve her distress.

He covered the distance between them in two swift strides and knelt beside her. Caution warned that the last time he'd gone down on his knees in her presence, it had not ended well. But its bleating alarm was drowned out by a roar of concern for Cassandra.

The sound of his footsteps made her glance up just as

he reached her. She gave a violent start at the sight of him. But when he opened his arms, she did not shrink from him. Instead, she flung herself into his embrace, her head pressed against his shoulder.

In that instant, every particle of tension that had built up inside of Brandon over the past four years seemed to melt away. The throttling grip around his throat released and he drew his first truly easy breath in a very long while.

"There now," he whispered, savoring the silken caress of her hair against his cheek. "What is the matter? What can I do to help?"

"N-nothing." All the tension that had bled out of Brandon seemed to soak into Cassandra and crystallize. She pulled away as abruptly as she had thrown herself at him, but not before Brandon inhaled her scent into the deepest recesses of his lungs. "I don't know what came over me."

She dashed the tears from her eyes as if she despised herself for giving in to them. "Perhaps I am overtired. I began thinking of my sisters and how worried they will be about me, especially Viola. I wish I could get a message to them that I am safe."

Brandon recalled Cassandra's gentle, fair-haired sister whom many considered the beauty of the Whitney family. Much as he admired the lady, he could not agree.

"I suppose Lady Viola must be married now." He took out his handkerchief and offered it to Cassandra. "Did Lord Gilchrist secure her or did she make a better match?"

After a moment's hesitation, Cassandra seized his handkerchief and dried her eyes with it. In answer to his question, she shook her head. "My sister is not married."

The information puzzled Brandon but the lady's tone did not encourage further inquiry.

Instead a different question burst out before he could prevent it. "Are you certain it was only the thought of your sisters that upset you? You looked troubled when I spoke about the war earlier. Forgive me. I did not mean to upset you. I should have held my tongue."

"No, you should not!" She glanced up at Brandon through her lush fringe of black lashes, to which tiny beads of moisture clung. That look penetrated his defenses with the force and precision of a well-aimed rifle shot.

"How can I shrink from hearing of your experiences in the war when you had the courage to endure them?" she continued. "What distressed me more than learning what you suffered was the thought that I might have pushed you into taking up a commission. Admit it — you would never have gone to war if I had accepted your marriage proposal."

Brandon was not without his own pride, which now urged him to deny the charge. Confessing to it would only betray the depth of his heartbreak. But how could he claim otherwise? Truth was a rigorous taskmaster, which demanded its due even when the tribute was not pleasant or convenient.

"That cannot come as any great surprise, surely?" He might not be able to refute her assertion outright, but he could try to make light of it. "What man with any sense would leave his bride to go off to war unless he was compelled to? If you had accepted my proposal, I would have been more agreeably employed beginning our married life together. But since I had no such ties to prevent me, I decided I should do my duty for King and Country."

That explanation sounded impersonal and almost noble. Brandon knew his decision had been neither. "Besides, there are few situations better calculated to make a fellow forget his romantic troubles than facing enemy fire."

His attempt at levity failed miserably.

Cassandra pressed his handkerchief to her lips. Though she managed to hold back a fresh effusion of weeping, her whole demeanor suggested misery too deep for tears.

"No wonder you hate me." She spat out the words as if they were choking her. "I drove you away to war. You might have been wounded, even ... k-killed and it would have been my fault."

"I do not hate you!" The vehement denial burst out before Brandon could judge whether or not it was true. But once he'd spoken, he realized he meant it. There was a time when he'd *tried* to hate Cassandra Whitney, but he had not succeeded. "Furthermore, any harm that might have come to me in Spain would have been the doing of Napoleon's army, not you."

His reassurances did not persuade her. "I might as well have pushed you in front of their bullets … or bayonets. If I had only known …"

At that moment Brandon could not abide the word *if.* It taunted him with too many images of what might have been.

"What would you have done?" He rose from the floor and stalked off to peer out the kitchen window. He did not trust himself so near Cassandra now that he'd been reminded how it felt to hold her in his arms. "If I had threatened to go to war unless you accepted my proposal, would you have given in to such blackmail? Would you have agreed to wed me in spite of your feelings, or lack of them? You would not have done either of us a service if you had. A union on that basis would have been doomed to the worst kind of failure."

Indeed it would. Yet, as he spoke with such conviction, Brandon wondered why he had never considered her refusal in that light until this moment. Though he had not been able to hate Cassandra, he had privately blamed her, just as she now blamed herself, for making him go to war.

That had been grossly unjust.

He alone was responsible for his actions, however reckless. He must do everything in his power to convince her of that. She might not have cared for him enough to risk marriage, particularly after watching her father make three wives miserable. Yet he now sensed that Cassandra had not been altogether indifferent to his fate either. She had worried about him and regretted any hardships he'd suffered. She did not deserve to carry the burden of his imprudent choices.

But before he had a chance to tell her any of that, she seized upon his final words. "What do you know about the worst kind of failure in a marriage? You told me this morning that having plenty of male heirs did not insure a happy family. Were you speaking from intimate observation, as I did last evening?"

Once, during a skirmish in a Spanish village, Brandon had been ambushed by a French infantryman. He would never forget the way the Iberian sun glinted off the muzzle of that Charleville musket aimed at his chest. The soft click of the flintlock hammer striking the frizzen had told him he would be dead before he could take any evasive action. By some miracle the weapon had misfired, giving him vital seconds to raise his like a club and knock the musket out of his enemy's hands.

Cassandra's question reminded him of that soft but ominous sound. Only this time he had no hope of a reprieve. Nor was he certain he deserved one.

Chapter Eight

S IR BRANDON CALVERT did not hate her for the way she had treated him? Cassandra's mind and heart dwelt on that improbable notion as she savored the sweet memory of his unexpected embrace.

How she had longed to surrender to it and cling to him for every last instant his kindness would permit. Pride had refused to let him see her so vulnerable. What if he'd sensed the feelings she once had for him — feelings she had been forced to deny for his sake? She could bear his contempt better than his pity. If he learned the truth, she would probably have to suffer both.

So she'd pulled away from him, pretending it was propriety that demanded such action, rather than pride. But neither of those things could make her forget the sensation of his arms encircling her, his broad shoulder offered to lean or weep upon, whichever she needed. Not to mention the provocative whisper of his warm breath through her hair.

Cassandra raised Brandon's handkerchief to her face, pretending to wipe away a tear. Instead she inhaled the faint scent of him that clung to the damp square of linen.

From her seat at the Martins' kitchen table, she watched Brandon stare out the tiny, frosted window into the night. The snow did not appear to be falling as hard as earlier, but neither had it stopped. Cassandra wished he would come back to kneel or sit beside her again. What had she said to drive him away? Whatever it was, she would gladly take it back.

Ah, yes. She had tried to assume the blame for driving him

away to war. Then she had mused aloud about how differently she might have acted if she'd foreseen the consequences of her refusal. For some reason, that seemed to vex him. Perhaps despite the way her rejection had wounded his pride, Brandon Calvert was not sorry to have escaped wedding her after all. If that were true then he might not care to be reminded of what his life could have been.

His reply had prompted her to ask about his family. Until now she had given no thought to what circumstances, other than an unbroken string of daughters, might destroy a marriage.

"I suppose I owe you an answer." Brandon continued to gaze out the window as if it held a sight of far greater interest than snowflakes dancing in the darkness. "After all, you gave me one to an equally personal question."

Cassandra held her tongue. She owed him more than he could ever owe her, but she still wanted to hear what he might say. When the time came for them to part again, at least she would have the minor consolation of knowing him a little better than she had before.

Brandon inhaled a deep breath then began to speak. His tone was wooden, as if he'd deliberately severed his emotions from his memories. "To the rest of the world, my parents' marriage must have appeared a brilliant match. But that is all it ever was — appearance. My mother wed my father for his fortune. He married her because her beauty and wit made her sought after by other men. She got the life of luxury that a bountiful income can provide and he became the envy of every gentleman of his acquaintance. But as the years went by, my parents came to realize they had paid too high a price for the advantages they'd gained."

Though he was not looking toward her, Cassandra nodded just the same. She understood the ultimate cost of a mercenary marriage. And yet, her family's present circumstances reminded her that such sacrifices might sometimes be necessary.

"By the time I was old enough to notice, my parents heartily despised one another," Brandon mused. "When one did address the other, which happened seldom, it was usually a bitter quip laced with poisonous hidden meaning. Only when they appeared in public together did they make an effort to behave as if all was well between them. Then their performances would have put Mr. Kemble and Mrs. Siddons to shame."

It was clear from his tone that Brandon did not approve of his parents cordial behavior in public. But Cassandra thought she understood why they had acted that way. Was it not bad enough to endure the private acrimony of their marriage? Being the subjects of gossip or objects of pity would have rubbed salt in the wounds.

She wanted to ask Brandon whether he would have preferred his father to make humiliating remarks about his mother in public, as she had seen hers do to poor Letty. But before she could get the words out, she heard the patter of footsteps approaching down the passage from the parlor.

Imogene Calvert flounced into the kitchen. "What are you doing Brandon, *pressing* apples for cider?"

Cassandra glanced from Miss Calvert to her cousin, puzzled.

"I came out to fetch more cider for myself and Mrs. Martin." Brandon explained before answering his cousin's question. "Lady Cassandra and I fell into conversation. Is that a crime? When did you become so concerned about the comfort of our hostess?"

"Don't be ridiculous." Miss Calvert sniffed. "You may talk all you like, only please do it in the parlor where I may join in the conversation. Nobody else there has anything to say that is of interest to me."

"You are quite right, Miss Calvert." Cassandra rose from the table. She and Brandon had been away from the rest of the party for longer than was proper. She did not care to become the subject of gossip. "I'm sure we would be much more comfortable carrying on our conversation in the parlor."

It would be impossible for them to discuss such personal subjects as they had been, but perhaps that was for the best. What good would come of talking about the past? What was done was done and no amount of conversation would change it.

"I'm certain you will, Lady Cassandra." Imogene Calvert locked arms with her and started back toward the parlor. "At least such comfort as may be found in a place like this."

"That is enough, Imogene." Brandon started after them with an air that seemed to mingle relief and regret. "We are fortunate to have found such a warm welcome here."

"I know. I know." His cousin heaved an impatient sigh. "Mr. and Mrs. Martin are very kind. It is warm and dry here and we have plenty to eat and drink. I am not as ungrateful as you believe. But you must admit, it lacks the refinements of Everleigh ... or Noughtly Hall. I do hope the weather will improve soon so we can all get to where we are meant to be."

She should want that too, Cassandra told herself. The longer she stayed in this house with Brandon, becoming more intimately acquainted than they had ever been, the harder it would be for her to part from him again. Yet no matter how often or how strenuously she reminded herself of that, part of her still wished the snow would not stop until Easter!

Brandon's cousin began waxing lyrical about the charms of Everleigh and the various guests who would be attending the Norrington's house party. She and Cassandra settled into the empty window seat. They were joined by her cousin after he had fetched Mrs. Martin her cider.

"Was it a *partner* in conversation you wished, Imogene, or an audience?" Brandon teased as he squeezed in beside his cousin. "You have scarcely given Lady Cassandra the opportunity to get a word in."

Miss Calvert made a face at him. "I did ask her about the festivities she expects to enjoy at Noughtly Hall. She said Everleigh sounded much more amusing. Then she asked me to tell her who else would be there. Isn't that right, Lady Cassandra?"

"Indeed it is." Cassandra tried to sound suitably interested in what Miss Calvert had to say. She would rather hear about the most tiresome subject in the world than tell the truth about her impending ordeal serving as a companion to her great-aunt. She did not want Brandon to know how far her fortunes had fallen, but neither did she dare try to make her visit to Noughtly sound more agreeable than it would be. Brandon seemed to possess a special intuition for detecting falsehood. Better to avoid the subject altogether.

"Your cousin tells me there will be quite a number of eligible ladies and gentleman attending the party," she continued. "I wish you good fortune in your mutual match-making endeavors, though I doubt you will need it. I am certain you will both have many admirers from whom to choose."

She made a determined effort not to let her smile falter as she pictured Brandon surrounded by a bevy of fawning ladies eager to make a conquest of him.

Miss Calvert appeared flattered by the compliment but her cousin's lip curled in a sneer. "I much prefer quality over quantity. If I am able to secure the sincere regard of one lady, I would rather have that than empty flirtations with half-a-dozen."

Though he spoke as if it were a general remark, Cassandra felt his contempt aimed directly at her. Clearly he believed she had felt nothing more for him than an empty flirtation. She had no right to take offense for that was precisely the impression she had sought to convey when she rejected his proposal. The sweet relief she'd experienced when Brandon assured her he did not hate her suddenly turned sour. No doubt he had meant she was not even worthy of his hatred.

Lady Cassandra wished him luck in finding a wife, even after he had held her in his arms and confessed one of the most painful secrets of his past? Could there be any clearer indication that she did not want him to get any foolish ideas that she cared for him?

She might not wish any harm to come to him. She might regret the possibility that her rejection had driven him to war. That did not mean she had developed tender feelings toward him … only a guilty conscience.

In response to his remark about preferring quality of romantic attention over quantity, Cassandra replied. "If the ladies possess sufficient sense and taste, I have no doubt at least one will lose her heart to you."

Was she patronizing him now — trying to reassure him that even though she had not been willing to wed him, others might be?

Brandon gave a self-deprecating shrug to show that he was not a child who needed to be coddled. "Perhaps they will have higher standards than you suppose. They may wonder why I remain a bachelor at my present age. They may suspect I am concealing some secret defect that would make me a thoroughly unsuitable husband."

His rebuff ignited a flash of indignation in her dark eyes. But Brandon glimpsed an unaccountable sparkle in them as well. "A woman who suspects you of *concealing* anything must not know you at all, Sir Brandon. Your insistence on strict truthfulness is the trait of yours I recall most clearly. I believe it is far more likely that no lady can hope to meet your high standards in that regard."

Was she mocking his values now? "I do not believe my standards are unreasonably high. I simply speak the truth and expect others to do likewise. It is an ideal everyone praises but few practice."

During their give and take, Imogene had looked as if she wanted to get a word in, but had not been able to. Now she settled back with her arms crossed to wait for their discussion to run its course.

"Everything cannot always be neatly divided between truth and falsehood." A flush rose in Lady Cassandra's cheeks and the lively sparkle in her eyes intensified.

Brandon wished he did not find the combination so very attractive. It gave the lady an unfair advantage in their debate.

"Of course it can," he insisted. "A statement may be true or not. If it is not, then it must be a falsehood. I do not believe it is too much to expect the truth."

His words provoked a subtle flinch, which Brandon noted with grim satisfaction. Lady Cassandra must realize their discussion was not as impersonal as it might sound. She was trying to justify her past behavior, which he could not help but condemn.

"Of course it is not unreasonable to prefer the truth." She leaned toward him as she spoke, which made Brandon realize he was leaning toward her as well. "I am only saying there are some things more important that the truth can damage with its sharp edges."

"What sorts of things?" He meant his question to sound doubtful, but instead it emerged curious and engaged.

"The feelings of others for one," Cassandra responded without hesitation. "Some of the most disagreeable people pride themselves on saying hurtful things because they are true."

"Whom do you mean?" Was she referring to him? Brandon could not decide whether he ought to be indignant or ashamed.

"My Aunt Augusta is a prime example," Lady Cassandra replied. "The moment she sets eyes on me, I know she will say I look every year of my age, and that I have gotten dreadfully thin of late."

"Nonsense!" The irate denial rose to Brandon's lips before he could stop it. "You scarcely seem to have aged a year since I saw you last and your slenderness is most becoming."

His observations were perfectly true, yet Brandon wished he had kept them to himself. Would Lady Cassandra assume he was trying to flatter her? He could not repent his words altogether, though. They brought a winsome, teasing smile to her face that made him catch his breath.

"You see? There is another difficulty." Her tone reminded Brandon of the way they had bantered with one another when they were first becoming acquainted. "Who would be telling the truth, you or my aunt? You might both believe what you say but a disinterested observer might see that neither of you is altogether correct."

"I am disinterested," he insisted. But when Cassandra fixed him with a doubtful look, he was forced to admit, "Perhaps not entirely. But what I said is true just the same."

Imogene appeared to be resting her eyes.

"I know you believe so," Cassandra conceded, "but Aunt Augusta would claim the same thing. Can two such different opinions both be true or neither? The matter is not as straightforward as you might like to believe."

She had a valid point, loathe as Brandon was to admit it.

He tried to salvage his position. "Perhaps when it comes to opinion, but not facts. Surely you can agree it is wrong to knowingly misrepresent them."

That made Cassandra squirm a little. Or perhaps she found the window seat uncomfortable with three of them squeezed in so tightly. Brandon glanced toward his cousin. Imogene's features had gone slack and her head lolled to one side. Her breath came in soft, rhythmic gusts.

He looked back at Cassandra, who gave a rueful grimace. Then the two of them chuckled softly.

"I fear our discourse was too tiresome for your poor cousin to abide." Cassandra glanced around to see if anyone else had noticed, but the rest of the party appeared engrossed in their own conversations.

"It was not tiresome." Brandon could not suppress a guilty grin, even though it contradicted his earnest declaration. "We were discussing a question of great moral significance about which we hold strong, opposing views. What could be more stimulating?"

Stimulating — how well that word described his debate

with Cassandra. Though parts of their exchange had reminded him how painfully she'd once trodden on his heart, it had also forced him to recall the pleasure he'd found in her company.

Caution and painful experience warned him to not draw too close to the woman who might still possess the power to make him suffer. But he chose to ignore them. He and Cassandra were presently chaperoned by more than half-a-dozen people. How much trouble could he get into with a little conversation?

"What indeed?" The lady replied, turning her gaze fully upon him.

Suddenly a great many provocative possibilities flashed through Brandon's mind, the most urgent of which was kissing her ripe, inviting lips. If they had been alone at that moment, he was not certain he could have resisted the temptation.

Perhaps Cassandra recognized how thoroughly she had thrown him off guard and sought to exploit the opportunity. "Last evening you suggested we try to forget the past and behave like new acquaintances. Would that not be a deception of sorts?"

"Um … er …" Brandon tugged at his neck linen. Uncomfortable as her question made him, he had to concede it might be true.

"In any case, I find I cannot do what you ask." She sounded apologetic but he could hardly blame her. He had not been able to do what he'd suggested either.

"This meeting between us was unlooked-for." She lowered her voice, forcing him to lean closer to hear her over the other conversations in the room.

"But perhaps it is an opportunity I should not neglect."

An opportunity for what? Brandon's eyebrows shot up in a silent question.

"To tell you how sorry I am for any injury I caused you when I refused your kind offer four years ago. I do not expect you to forgive me but I want to make certain you understand it was no fault of yours that prompted my answer. Any lady would be fortunate to secure you as a husband."

Brandon knew he must make some reply but he feared anything he said at the moment would sound ridiculous.

Her words revived bitter memories he'd worked hard to bury. He recalled the sweet urgency that had compelled him to seek a private word with Cassandra Whitney. Once again he tasted the intoxicating hope that she would ensure his happiness by agreeing to share a future with him. In spite of his dark doubts about marriage, his feelings for Cassandra had filled him with naïve optimism that their union could be different.

He'd gone down on his knees like a besotted supplicant and offered her his heart. For an instant he thought he'd glimpsed an answering glimmer of tenderness in her eyes. But that must have been a wishful delusion. She had immediately turned haughty and aloof, an ice maiden without an ember of warmth or soft emotion within her.

"You have been a most amusing companion, sir." The memory of her heartless rejection returned to smite Brandon. "But surely you cannot be serious about proposing. If I led you to believe my feelings for you were more than they are, I beg your pardon. But I simply cannot marry you."

Every word from her bewitching lips had mocked his foolish hopes in the face of all his experience to the contrary. Later he'd tried to make peace with her rejection. He told himself it was better she had turned him down rather than accepting his proposal for the wrong reasons. That would have doomed them to repeat his parents' mistakes.

His attempt to rationalize away his heartbreak had not been as successful as he wished, but it was better than nothing.

"Any *other* lady, you mean," he muttered when he'd recovered his voice. Inwardly he cringed at his tone, which betrayed far too much about unhealed wounds.

"*Any* lady," Cassandra repeated with a mixture of defiance and regret. "I have no doubt you would have been a far better husband than I deserved. My only consolation is that I left you free to find the kind of wife who is worthy of you."

Did she mean that? Brandon could not reconcile the unfeeling girl of his memories with the sweetly contrite lady before him.

"I cannot blame you if you do not believe me," she continued. "I was a thoughtless, selfish child and I treated you very badly. If it is any consolation, I have come to regret my actions most bitterly. I would repent them even more if my refusal drove you into the army and prevented you from finding a wife."

Brandon opened his mouth to deny it, in part because he did not want to make her feel worse and also because it made him sound so insufferably pathetic. But before he could summon the words to soothe her conscience and salve his pride, he realized they would not be true. How could he lie to her after his self-righteous lecture about the vital importance of telling the truth?

"You need not fret about that. As I told you earlier, my actions are my own responsibility. If I was foolish enough to react so excessively, it is not your fault." The notion stung him in a sensitive place that had already been chafed by the revival of painful memories. The only way to ease his discomfort was to vent it outward. "Besides, it was not your *refusal* that grieved me but rather the way you encouraged me to believe you cared for me in the first place."

That *was* the worst part. Over the years Brandon told himself so whenever old memories rose too close to the surface. He had not resented Cassandra for breaking his heart. He had resented her for tricking him into giving it to her in the first place. And he despised himself even more for being so gullible when he had every reason to be on his guard.

"Quibble all you wish," he concluded, "I do not believe you can justify that deception."

Brandon expected his accusation to provoke a look of shame or regret from her. Perhaps anger with him for shining a harsh light upon the wrong she'd done him. He was not prepared for a gaze of mute suffering, as if *she* were the one whose heart had been broken by her refusal to wed him.

He had long prided himself on his ability to tell when someone was trying to deceive him. In that moment, he knew without a doubt Cassandra was not.

"You *did* care for me?" he whispered, as if fearful of waking some large, predatory creature.

Her head jerked up and down in the most reluctant admission. Part of Brandon wanted to doubt her, but he could not.

Did he dare ask the question that cried out in his mind and his heart? If Cassandra had cared for him, what could have made her refuse his proposal?

Chapter Nine

WHAT HAD POSSESSED her to confess her true feelings to Brandon Calvert after four long years? That question throbbed in Cassandra's mind as she watched a bewildering variety of emotions flicker in his candid blue eyes.

The other conversations around them seemed to fade, as if coming from a much farther distance. The thunder of her heartbeat nearly drowned them out.

Had she dared to tell Brandon the truth at last because she'd assumed he would not believe her? If so, it was a grave miscalculation. She had given him ample cause to doubt her. But the new closer connection they had formed during the past two days seemed to have given him clearer insight into her motives and emotions. She glimpsed a brief flicker of uncertainty in his eyes, but other reactions swiftly overpowered it.

Now that he knew the truth, Cassandra feared he would not rest until he had uncovered all her secrets. What would happen then?

"I do not understand." Brandon shook his head, his features contracted like those of a young scholar trying to work out a difficult sum. "If that is true, then why …?"

"Why what?" Imogene Calvert woke from her convenient doze, perhaps not even aware that she'd nodded off. "I vow, you two are quite as bad as the others, talking on and on about subjects of no interest to me."

Under other circumstances, Cassandra might have been annoyed that Brandon's cousin had interrupted their private conversation. At the moment, however, she was overcome with relief. She was under no illusion that Brandon would let the matter drop with his curiosity unsatisfied. At least this interruption would give her a chance to regain her composure before they spoke about the subject again.

"Lord and Lady Norrington are well-known for their hospitality," Miss Calvert informed Cassandra, not for the first time. "Have you ever been a guest at Everleigh?"

"I have not had that pleasure." She tried to concentrate all her attention on Brandon's cousin, to avoid his penetrating gaze. "Since our father's death, my sisters and I have lived rather quietly in the country with our stepmother."

"You mustn't rusticate forever," Miss Calvert warned her. "You could still find a perfectly tolerable husband, provided you are not too particular. But if you delay much longer your prospects will not improve."

"Imogene!" her cousin thundered. "Have you no manners at all? You should apologize to Lady Cassandra at once."

Some of the others glanced toward the window seat when Brandon raised his voice. They quickly looked away again and raised the volume of their conversations.

"You are a fine one to talk about manners," Miss Calvert huffed. "I thought you only cared about everyone telling the truth. That is what you were lecturing poor Lady Cassandra about. Did I say a single word that was untrue?"

"Perhaps … not strictly," he muttered, clearly agitated. "But there is a time to exercise discretion."

Cassandra could not help but be amused to watch the baronet scramble to defend a position he had so recently attacked. "Do not fret, Sir Brandon. I am not offended. What your cousin says *is* true. At my age, I am unlikely to find a husband unless I make a good deal more effort."

She did not mention having had other opportunities to wed, if she'd been so inclined. But after rejecting the one man she truly wanted for a husband, how could she accept anyone else?

Having twitted her cousin about being inconsistent in his

views, Imogene Calvert soon returned to her favorite topic. "Lord Norrington's ward, Miss Willis will be there, of course. That is how I came to be invited. We have been friends since we were little girls. She is hoping to get *better acquainted* with Mr. Reynolds, whose sister—"

Brandon interrupted his cousin in a sharp tone. "You complain of everyone else discussing subjects that do not interest you. Yet you do not consider whether Lady Cassandra wishes to hear every detail about a group of people she does not know or care about."

It was not like him to be quite so peremptory. Cassandra wondered if he was still vexed with his cousin for her earlier comments.

"How can you be so certain she does not know any of Lord Norrington's guests?" Miss Calvert demanded. "I did not realize *you* were previously acquainted with Lady Cassandra. How did you come to know her, by the way?"

His cousin's question clearly caught Brandon off guard, Cassandra sensed when he hesitated to reply. He must not want her to know the precise nature of their connection for fear she might pester him with more inquiries. Or perhaps he feared she would try to play Cupid between them. Much as he might wish to avoid either of those things, he would not want to be less than truthful with his cousin, either.

Before Brandon's prolonged silence raised his cousin's suspicion, Cassandra answered on behalf of them both. "Sir Brandon and I had several friends in common, so we frequently found ourselves invited to the same assemblies when my family came to London."

She cast him a pointed glance to indicate this was how one exercised truthful discretion. He answered with a wry half-smile that managed to covey a measure of gratitude.

Cassandra's reply seemed to satisfy Miss Calvert's curiosity for she made no further inquiries about the nature of their acquaintance. Instead, she returned to the subject of the Everleigh house party. This time, Brandon did not interrupt or chide her. He must have realized there were worse things she might chatter on about.

As the evening drew to a close, Cassandra began to hope Brandon might have forgotten her earlier admission of her past feelings for him.

But as the company rose to retire for the night, he brushed past her, close enough to whisper, "We have matters to discuss, you and I. I shall be waiting for you in the kitchen early tomorrow morning."

When she gave no reply except a look of alarm, he added, "Surely I deserve an explanation."

His words echoed in her thoughts as she followed the other women upstairs and helped his cousin get ready for bed. Cassandra could not deny them. Brandon had admitted he would not have gone to war if she had accepted his proposal. That made her guilty of placing him in danger, no matter what he might say to the contrary.

That did not mean it would be easy to look him in the eye and explain why she'd acted as she had. At the time, she'd believed it was the right choice for both of them. Now she was not so certain.

Her doubts kept her awake that night as much as Imogene Calvert kicking her shins and stealing the bedclothes. At least the wind had stopped moaning around the eaves, but that was little comfort under the circumstances.

Finally, when Cassandra could no longer bear another minute of tossing and turning, she slipped out of bed, fumbled into her clothes and crept downstairs. The kitchen was dark and deserted when she reached it. A handful of glowing embers still smoldered in the grate. She swept out the ashes and kindled a new fire from the remains of the old. Warming her hands before the small blaze she waited for the kettle to boil.

The water was still only simmering when Brandon wandered in. He wiped the sleep from his eyes then stretched his long limbs and gave a deep yawn. "I did not expect to find you here before me. In fact, I was not certain you would come at all until the kitchen was full of chaperones."

Cassandra shrugged. "I could not sleep so I decided I might as well be up. I cannot pretend I am eager for this interview, but you were right when you said I owe you an explanation. I fear I owe you a great deal more than that, but it is all I have to offer at the moment. "

It might have been easier to face him if he did not look so ruggedly attractive. He had not shaved in two days and now a dark stubble of whisker bristled from his sharply-etched jaw. His golden brown hair was rumpled in a way that made her hand itch to smooth it down then linger in a fond caress. His eyes had lost their direct, uncompromising stare. Instead they held a weary, bewildered look that was dangerously endearing.

Against her will, Cassandra's hand crept up to the loose plait of hair that hung over her shoulder. She could imagine how disheveled it must look and how pasty her complexion. The smudges of exhaustion beneath her eyes would complete the pitiful picture. Her pride smarted at having him see her like this when he looked so wretchedly appealing.

"You are no coward, I'll say that for you." Brandon fetched himself a kitchen chair and placed it beside hers in front of the fire. "Now, before we are interrupted, kindly explain to me why you refused my marriage proposal if you did care for me after all?"

Cassandra's stomach churned and her mouth went dry. How could she begin to explain in a way he might understand? Brandon had claimed he did not hate her for refusing him four years ago. Would he still be able to make that claim once she told him the truth? And would she ever be able to look him in the face once he heard what her father had intended to do?

Lady Cassandra Whitney did not look much like the daughter of a duke as she hunched before a cottage fire, warming her hands and pushing a stray lock of hair off her forehead. Yet she had an air of intrepid integrity Brandon could not deny.

She was prepared to tackle a task she shrank from because she believed it was the right thing to do.

Why had she chosen to deceive him regarding her feelings? Until last night, he thought she had only pretended to care for him before cruelly rejecting him. Now it seemed her feelings for him had been true while her denial of them had been false. Whichever it had been should not matter. A lie was a lie and could not be excused, especially when it concerned matters of the heart.

Brandon had learned than harsh lesson from his family. However since his recent discussions with Cassandra, he was less certain of his long-held belief.

"Well?" he prompted her when she hesitated to answer his question. "Why did you refuse my proposal and make me believe you were only trifling with my affections if you did care for me? I tried all night to imagine a reason. Was it because of your father? Were you afraid I would treat you unkindly after we were married? Did you think I only wanted a broodmare to provide me with an heir?"

Much as he wanted to resent Cassandra believing him capable of either, Brandon found he could not. Hadn't he been quick to judge her as heartless and deceitful as his mother, even though she'd given him no prior reason to assume such a thing?

What might have happened if he had not rushed to condemn her four years ago? What if he had questioned her more closely, rather than storming away? If he'd been more understanding, might it have shown Cassandra he would not be the kind of husband her father had been? Then perhaps she would have reconsidered her decision and they could have made a life together … raised a family.

A tantalizing vision rose in his mind of them celebrating Twelfth Night in their own home. A Yule log crackled on the hearth and a handsomely-decked kissing bough hung in the sitting room. He pictured himself bouncing a vivacious, dark-haired little daughter on his knee while Cassandra cradled their infant son.

When she began to speak, stirring him from his musing, Brandon returned to the present with a heart-wrenching jolt. How could he miss so acutely something he'd never had and perhaps never would? He tried to comfort himself by imaging a family he might have with Isabella Reynolds, but it was only a cold abstraction, not real to him like the other had been.

Cassandra shook her head. "I knew you were nothing like my father in that regard. But it was on account of him that I refused your proposal, when my heart urged me to accept. You see, there was another reason my father married the women he did, besides his quest to sire an heir."

"What reason?" The question emerged in a gruff tone Brandon had not intended. He was only trying to keep his voice steady after hearing her admit she'd wanted to marry him.

"The root of all evil." Cassandra refused to meet his gaze. Instead she stared into the fire as if it held the answer to any question he might pose. "My father was a proud man — the heir to a dukedom from the moment of his birth. He grew up believing he was entitled to whatever his heart desired. My grandfather was wise enough to realize it would ruin the family to indulge him in that way, so he gave Father a modest allowance and told him he must learn to live within his means."

Her account puzzled Brandon for two reasons. "I agree that your grandfather adopted a wise course. But your family always appeared to live well. In any case, I do not see what bearing this has on our situation."

"Indulge me a moment and it will become clear," she murmured. "My father did live as well as he believed he deserved, off the fortunes of his wives. It would seem he and your mother had a similar view of matrimony. The difference was that the women who wed him believed they were marrying for love, poor creatures."

Brandon still could not fathom why any of that had made Cassandra decline his proposal.

"Father's first two wives obliged him by dying before he

had run through their entire fortunes. Letty did not. By the time my sisters and I came out in Society, Father was deeply in debt, though we did not realize it. Did you never wonder why he discouraged Viscount Gilchrist and Lord Alanham from courting my sisters, while he looked favorably on my connection with a baronet?"

"It did occur to me," Brandon admitted, feeling like a fool for being so blind to her father's deception. "I thought it might be a measure of how well he believed you and I would suit one another. I assumed he valued me for more than my title."

"He did indeed." Cassandra heaved a dry, mirthless chuckle. "My father weighed you in the balance and found the size of your fortune more than compensated for what he considered the inferiority of your rank."

She turned her head to look Brandon in the eye. "I had no idea what he intended to do. I realize I have given you little reason to believe me, but I swear by everything I hold dear, I did not know. Not until the evening before you proposed to me."

Brandon knew what she wanted him to say. Though he could not resist the appeal that glimmered in her dark eyes, his need to learn the whole story was more urgent still. He could not be certain how many more minutes they might have alone. "What exactly did your father plan to do? Did he mean to make me *purchase* his consent for our marriage?"

Cassandra's head drooped. "Perhaps that is how it would have begun. Then it would have been something else, and something more after that. It would not have stopped until he was in his grave or your fortune was exhausted. I overheard him telling Letty when she begged him to allow Viola to accept Lord Gilchrist. Father told her Vi should follow my example and find a beau with the capacity to assist our family. I knew then that if I agreed to marry you, his hand would always be in your pocket. I could not let him ruin you."

Brandon believed her. How could he not? He had witnessed firsthand that kind of selfishness. If his family's fortune had been exhausted he could easily picture his mother urging him to seek a rich wife for her sake.

But there was something else he found impossible to fathom.

"Why did you not tell me all this four years ago?" he demanded. "Why did you refuse my proposal and pretend it was because you did not care for me?"

Her head snapped up. She shot him a defiant glare. "I was trying to protect you! I did not want my father to bleed you dry the way he did my mother and my stepmothers."

"What made you so certain he would have?" Part of Brandon understood that she had acted out of concern for him. But his pride bristled at the thought that he might need to be protected. "A woman would be vulnerable to such exploitation once she married a man who had designs on her fortune. It would come under his control from the moment they wed. I would not have been bound that way, especially if you warned me what your father meant to do."

Cassandra's glare collapsed into a dazed stare, as if she had been clouted on the head, not quite hard enough to knock her out. "But … but … you do not know what he was like. Father could be very charming and persuasive when he wanted something. He would not have hesitated to play upon your feelings for me, and mine for my sisters. You would have grown to hate me for bringing all our troubles into your life. I could not bear to let that happen."

Brandon shook his head. He sensed Cassandra believed what she was telling him. But he suspected there might have been more to it than she realized. Sometimes the worst deception was the kind people practiced upon themselves. "Yet you were willing to risk my hatred by rejecting my proposal out of the blue."

Cassandra winced. "I'd hoped it would not come to that. Once I knew what Father had planned, I meant to discourage you gradually, perhaps pick a quarrel so you would turn your attention to someone else. When you surprised me with your proposal, I could not think what else to do. I did not suppose you would take my rejection so hard. I was trying to spare you from ruin!"

"Were you?" The loss of the family he'd imagined for them still pained Brandon to a ridiculous degree. "Or were you trying to protect yourself from having to air your family's dirty linen? Were you afraid that if I learned the truth, I might spurn you? That would never do for the proud Miss Whitney, would it?"

Cassandra sprang from her chair. Her slender hands balled into tight fists. Much as Brandon wanted to nurse his righteous indignation toward her as a shield for his heart, he could not deny she looked magnificent. She inhaled a sharp breath and opened her mouth to roundly denounce him.

But before she could produce a single word, Brandon raised a forefinger to his lips and nodded toward the passage-way, down which he heard footsteps approaching.

As Mr. and Mrs. Martin entered the kitchen, Cassandra turned her attention to the kettle, which was steaming away vigorously.

"Did I not tell you, Tobias?" Mrs. Martin gestured toward Brandon and Cassandra. "Such a pair of early birds I never did see."

"Not a bad way to be either." Mr. Martin hooked his thumbs through his braces. "As that American saying goes — early to bed and early to rise ..."

Brandon forced a dry chuckle. "I am in good health and I have a comfortable fortune though it is inherited for the most part. The best I can say is that I have not frittered it all away."

"That leaves only wisdom, Sir Brandon." The sound of Cassandra's voice startled him though it should not have. "Surely you must admit to that."

Was she mocking him, after the things she had just confessed? Brandon pictured himself like Mrs. Martin's kettle, with his insides all hot and agitated as a scalding head of steam gathered. "I do not presume to praise my own understanding."

"Perhaps not," she replied as she filled the teapot, "But you have such decided opinions about how other people should behave. Why would you wish to dictate their actions, unless you believe that your way is always wiser and better?"

Her insincere smile reminded him of his mother's when the family was out in public — pretending maternal concern when she could scarcely bring herself to look at him in the privacy of their home.

"I must disagree." Brandon strove to keep his tone cool and light when the emotions brewing within him were quite the opposite. "I do not make any claim to wisdom. I have done a number of very foolish things in my life."

Tobias Martin clapped him on the back. "You did foolish things when you were young, Sir Brandon? I scarcely know a soul who hasn't. Human nature, that is. As long as you recognize your folly and learned your lesson, I reckon that's how you grow wise over the years."

The farmer's views were sound, charitable and thoroughly honest, just like his character.

"You are correct, sir," Brandon answered Mr. Martin but his words were aimed at Lady Cassandra Whitney. "I committed a number of very foolish errors in my youth, but at least I learned my lesson from them."

Chapter Ten

Finally! After four years she had her answer at last.

As Cassandra bustled around the kitchen, helping Mrs. Martin prepare breakfast, she exerted herself to look and sound cheerful. Not for a moment would she give Sir Brandon Calvert the satisfaction of guessing how downcast her spirits truly were.

His seemingly off-hand comment to Mr. Martin, about having made youthful mistakes and learned his lesson, ran through her thoughts over and over. Each time it struck her heart a blow.

Hardly a day had passed since she'd watched him stalk away, humiliated by her rejection, that she had not wondered how he might have reacted if he'd known the truth. Often her imagination had taunted her with rose-colored fancies of what Brandon might do if he learned that she had sacrificed her happiness to protect him from ruin.

When this terrible storm had thrown them together so unexpectedly, her curiosity about what might have been intensified into an insatiable need to know. It had goaded her into casting aside her pride to reveal the shameful truth about her family. Looking back, Cassandra wondered if she had been laying a foundation to help him understand why she'd been forced to refuse him.

At first it seemed to succeed. When Brandon had shared his family secrets, she'd felt a deeper connection between them than ever. She wondered if they had somehow sensed that common bond from the very beginning of their acquaintance.

Brandon's assurance that he did not hate her had given her further hope.

Hope for what? Cassandra sliced a loaf of bread with fierce vigor, relieved to have some vent for the tumultuous emotions swirling and churning inside her. Had she been daft enough to think Brandon would sweep her into his arms and confess that he had never stopped loving her? Did she imagine he would recognize the harm she had tried to spare him and cherish the sacrifice she'd made on his behalf?

Instead, when she'd confessed her most painful secret at last, Brandon had crushed her ridiculous hopes. He'd ignored everything but the fact that she had not been entirely truthful with him. Did he not realize how impossible that had been for her?

For an instant, Cassandra permitted her mask of cheerful industry to slip long enough to aim a baleful glare at the back of Brandon's head. Did he have so high an opinion of his own strength of will that he believed he could withstand her father's machinations to safeguard his fortune and their marriage? Cassandra knew better.

Such thoughts stoked her indignation the way she might have added fuel to Mrs. Martin's kitchen fire, making it burn fiercer and hotter. It protected her against the cold desolation of her quenched hopes and the icy sting of knowing Brandon considered their relationship a youthful folly, which he repented.

He claimed to have learned his lesson from that mistake. But what was that lesson? Never to trust a woman again? Never to give his heart? Vexed as Cassandra was with him, those possibilities still grieved her.

Gradually the smells of food drew the rest of the party to the kitchen.

When Mrs. Davis appeared, she immediately approached Cassandra. "Miss Calvert would like you to help her get dressed. I offered my services but she has her heart set on you."

No doubt so she could boast to her fellow guests at

Everleigh of having had a duke's daughter act as her lady's maid. Cassandra was tempted to say Miss Calvert could dress herself or stay in her nightgown. But tending to Brandon's cousin would give her a legitimate excuse to leave the kitchen, where she would have no choice but to see and hear him.

"Take all the time you need, my dear." Mrs. Martin waved her off. "I can manage here."

Only when she headed out of the kitchen did Cassandra realize Sir Brandon was standing near the passageway to the parlor. She would have to brush past him in order to leave the room. Refusing to be intimidated, she marched toward him with her spine stiff and her head high. As she approached, he started to move out of her way but Cassandra stepped toward him, as he had toward her the night before. Let him see how well *he* liked being ambushed!

"Perhaps I wasn't anxious to air my family's dirty linen," she muttered quietly enough for his ears alone. "But neither were you, as I recall."

With an intrepid toss of her head, she swept past him, desperate to get away before he could reply.

She was halfway to the parlor when she heard him call after her in a quiet but insistent voice, "Cassandra."

Her emotions were too stormy just then to risk arguing with him. If she tried, Cassandra feared she might give way to a foolish burst of tears. Not for anything would she let him see her weep again, now that she knew what he thought of her,

Instead she whirled around and robbed his accusations of their power by making them hers. "Perhaps I *should* have told you about my father. Perhaps I should have been entirely truthful about everything. But all I could think of was protecting you and that was the only way I could be certain. I made a mistake, but like you I have learned from it. In future, I will not do anything so foolish again."

She should have taken grim satisfaction in the look that gripped his features in response to her outburst. But she could not. It reminded her far too much of the heartbreaking mixture of shook, bewilderment and anguish she'd glimpsed on his face when she refused his proposal of marriage.

As she turned and rushed away, Cassandra feared Brandon might come after her and continue to rake up their troubled past. But by the time she reached the stairs, it was clear he had no intention of following her after all. The relief she expected to feel was accompanied by a contrary pang of disappointment.

She marched up the stairs to the little room she shared with the other ladies. Its space was further cramped by the presence of their luggage, which had been wrestled up the stairs the previous evening. Despite her protest that she would rather wear the same dress for a month than send the men out in the storm, Cassandra decided she would change into clean clothes once she had dressed and groomed Miss Calvert. For however long she was forced to remain in Sir Brandon's company, pride demanded that she make her best possible appearance.

"Is everything alright?" Imogene Calvert asked when Cassandra entered. "You look vexed. Are you sorry you offered to assist me? You must think I am a dreadful goose not to be able to dress myself."

A polite denial rose to Cassandra's lips, but she could imagine what Sir Brandon would say about that. The fact that she was displeased with the baronet did not make him wrong. The world might well be a better place, if people made an effort to speak and act more truthfully.

"I am not angry with you. But for your own wellbeing, it might be helpful for you to cultivate more independence. One cannot always be certain of having servants on hand." She congratulated herself on being perfectly truthful without insulting or distressing Sir Brandon's cousin.

Imogene Calvert seemed deaf to the important message Cassandra was trying to convey. She wrapped a blanket around her like a shawl and crawled out of bed. When her feet came in contact with the cold floor, she let out a pitiful squeal.

"If you aren't vexed with me" she persisted, "then whom?

Brandon?"

That was a far more difficult question to answer truthfully, for Cassandra feared it would provoke a flood of others. "We … er … we did have a difference of opinion but I would prefer not to discuss it. Now which dress do you wish to wear today? I would suggest one with long sleeves as it is quite cool."

Miss Calvert peered into the case, but once again she seemed to have heard only part of what Cassandra had said. "A difference of opinion? Are you referring to your debate last night? I've never seen Brandon so deeply engrossed in a conversation. Most of the time he only seems to half-listen to what other people say."

It must be a family trait, Cassandra concluded.

"You and my cousin seem to have a much closer acquaintance than I realized." Miss Calvert mused. Then she gave a violent start. "Oh my!"

"What is the matter?" Cassandra seized the young lady's hand, fearing she might be about to swoon. "Perhaps you should sit down on the bed for a moment."

"I am perfectly well, thank you." Imogene Calvert pushed Cassandra's hand away. "I only just realized who you must be."

"I beg your pardon?" What was the silly creature talking about? "You have known who I am ever since we met in the stagecoach."

Was that only two days ago? So much had happened since then, it seemed much longer.

"That is not what I mean!" Imogene Calvert snapped, as if she suspected Cassandra of being deliberately thickheaded. "Are you the woman who broke my cousin's heart?"

Cassandra wished she could deny the accusation, just as she had denied the truth to herself since the day she'd refused Brandon's proposal. It had been hard enough to live with herself when she thought she'd only injured his *pride* with her rejection.

"I … I did not mean to." How humiliating it was to be an object of disdain from a person for whom she had so little respect. "I did not believe he cared about me enough that my refusal would hurt him so much."

Miss Calvert's lip curled. She moved away from Cassandra as if she feared being contaminated. "He cared enough to make you an offer of marriage. I suppose you thought a baronet was not good enough for the daughter of a duke."

"Quite the contrary." It felt strange to be chastised by someone younger than her. Yet Cassandra was hard-pressed to defend herself from charges she feared she deserved. "My father had not inherited his title then."

That was a meaningless quibble, her conscience protested. As heir to a dukedom, her father had been highly conscious of his rank. He had discouraged her sisters from receiving the attentions of a viscount and a baron. Only Brandon Calvert's fortune had rendered him an acceptable suitor in her father's eyes.

It had been difficult enough to confess the true reason for her refusal to Brandon himself. Cassandra could not bear to reveal it to Imogene Calvert, who might spread the gossip far and wide. That would make the Whitney sisters objects of pity from all quarters. It might spoil Evie's chances of ever finding a husband.

Miss Calvert paid no more heed to Cassandra's feeble excuse than it deserved. "I suppose now that you are doomed to spinsterhood because you were too particular, you have decided you might stoop to take up with Brandon after all."

Cassandra shook her head vigorously but she could not summon the words to deny the charge. Of course she had not set her cap for Sir Brandon because he might be her last chance at wedlock. Yet she could not deny having harbored a foolish hope that once he discovered the true reason for her rejection, he might be able to forgive her and perhaps even learn to care for her again.

Their recent encounter had dashed that ridiculous delusion once and for all. Brandon had seemed more inclined to forgive her when he thought she was only dallying with him. He did not view her actions as the selfless sacrifice she'd intended but rather as an insult to his strength of will.

At first, his response had hurt and angered her. But the more she thought about it, the more she began to see the matter from his perspective. How might she have reacted if she learned that Brandon had ended their courtship without consulting her for reasons he believed to be in her best interests?

"You may save your flattery and your flirtatious banter!" Miss Calvert's eyes narrowed. "Brandon has found a much more suitable object for his affections. I am quite certain he intends to propose to her at Everleigh. No doubt Miss Reynolds will be sensible enough to accept him straight away."

It took every drop of Cassandra's considerable willpower to maintain her composure. "I am pleased to hear it. Your cousin deserves all the happiness life can bestow. It is all I have ever wanted for him."

The last part of her declaration was quite true. Cassandra hoped it might compensate for the bold-faced lie with which she'd begun. "Now shall I help you dress before you catch a chill?"

It was clear Imogene Calvert did not believe a word Cassandra had said, perhaps because her countenance betrayed her dismay.

The young lady looked down her nose at Cassandra. "I believe I can manage on my own after all, if I might trouble you to allow me a little privacy."

"Of course," Cassandra replied, equally stiff and correct. "If that is what you wish."

As much as Miss Calvert's contempt distressed her, she could not resent it. She might have behaved the same way to anyone she believed had insulted and hurt Brandon.

"Is breakfast not to your liking, Sir Brandon?" asked Mrs. Martin as most of the party tucked into the meal with hearty appetites. "I expect you must be accustomed to daintier fare."

Brandon roused from his brooding with a guilty start. "No

indeed, ma'am. During my army service, I was often lucky to get a morning bite of any kind. I would have been overjoyed to partake of such an excellent repast."

To convince her of his sincerity, he shoveled a spoonful of fried egg into his mouth and smiled broadly while he chewed and swallowed it. The effort nearly choked him.

He imagined this polite performance might make Cassandra question his truthfulness and suggest he should practice what he preached. But it was quite true that Mrs. Martin had prepared a fine breakfast, he assured his conscience. It was not her fault he was too preoccupied to appreciate it properly.

"You look as if you have a great deal on your mind," said Mrs. Martin, in a clear invitation to unburden himself.

Brandon might have considered it if there had not been a table full of other people present. "So I do, ma'am. I am wondering how long this storm will continue and we shall have to impose upon your generous hospitality."

That was *one* of the concerns occupying his thoughts. As Brandon made an effort to look as if he enjoyed the meal, the greater part of his mind continued to dwell on the things Cassandra had told him. Her surprising confession had turned his whole conception of her upside down. Nothing was as he'd believed it to be. When he recalled the day she had refused his proposal, his new insights into her family and her feelings seemed to illuminate his memories. They allowed him to perceive that painful event with true clarity at last.

He reflected on the wasted years he and Cassandra could have spent together, if only she'd had faith in him to stand up to her father. It made every muscle in his body clench and his fist itch to strike something.

His own face, perhaps? He was beginning to wonder if he deserved it.

Cassandra might have lost them the past four years together, but had he forfeited all the years to come? Perhaps she had made an unwise decision four years ago, but she had acted out of concern for him. His masculine pride resented the idea that she had acted without his knowledge in order to protect him. Would he not have done the same for her, though, if he'd been convinced that marrying him would harm her somehow?

He knew her father had been a man like any other, not some irresistible nemesis with the power to leech his fortune and poison their happiness. Together, they could have stood up to him. If he had proved too great a threat, they could have dismissed him from their lives.

But how could he expect Cassandra to take such an objective view? Brandon knew from experience the irrational, destructive power a malevolent parent could wield. Would he have been able to make light of the harm his mother could have done if she chose?

He needed to talk to Cassandra again, to explain why he'd reacted as he did. He needed to discover whether the feelings she'd once had for him were entirely a thing of the past, or whether they had persisted in spite of her efforts to quell them. What he needed most was *time* with her — time to get reacquainted, to catch up on their years apart. They needed to tell each other more about their early life, which had not always been kind to them.

But first he needed time to persuade her to speak to him again.

Preoccupied with his thoughts, Brandon scarcely noticed Tobias Martin rise from his chair and walk over to the kitchen window.

After standing awhile, peering out toward the well and fields beyond, he spoke. "You needn't wonder how long the storm will last, Sir Brandon. The snow looks to have stopped. It may take awhile to get the road cleared for coach traffic, but if the weather warms up, you might be surprised how quickly everything can get back to the way it should be."

The farmer's hopeful prediction had the opposite effect on Brandon's spirits. It appeared the one thing he needed most — time with Cassandra — might become a very scarce commodity.

Mrs. Martin seemed nearly as dismayed by the prospect of their departure as Brandon felt. "Surely our guests won't go away before we've celebrated Twelfth Night this evening. I planned to bake a cake, roast a goose and all."

"I hate to put you to so much trouble." Brandon replied. "I can only speak for my own party, but I believe we shall be obliged to enjoy your hospitality for one more night."

Now that the snow had stopped, they could likely make their way into the village and put up at the inn. But he would much rather stay here to celebrate Twelfth Night.

Mrs. Martin's obvious pleasure at Brandon's announcement eased any obligation he might feel for continuing to impose upon her and her husband.

"That's at least four guests I can count on." Their hostess turned to the stagecoach driver, who was seated on her left. "What about your lot? Will you be able to stay one more night or will you have to go?"

Brandon fixed the burly, red-faced man with a concentrated stare, willing him to stay put one more night. He would be prepared to part with a substantial bribe, if necessary to persuade the fellow.

The driver smiled at their hostess — a good sign, surely. "If there was nothing to consider but my own inclination, ma'am, I should be pleased to stay over, for I cannot recall when I've met a warmer reception. But I know my employers will expect me to press on if at all possible. There may be folks waiting for us at the stops ahead and I reckon my passengers are anxious to reach their destination."

Were they? Brandon wondered. Mrs. Davis seemed content to linger, having found a new friend in their hostess. But what about Cassandra? A few hours ago she might not have objected to remaining here. She might even have tried to persuade their driver. Now Brandon feared otherwise.

His only hope might be if she had taken the opportunity

to think matters over, as he had, and let her temper cool. Then perhaps she might begin to understand his excessive reaction to her recent revelations. He wondered if she and Imogene might have talked about him and his cousin might have put in a good word. If so, there could still be a chance for them to begin sorting out their differences before they must part ways.

Brandon had almost made himself believe it was possible when Imogene entered the kitchen. At the sight of her, his jaw dropped and conversation around the table fell into awkward silence.

His cousin looked a fright. Her dress hung at an odd angle, the cause of which he was at a loss to guess. That might not have drawn so much notice if her hair had been arranged in a neat, becoming style. Instead, it looked as if a flock of small birds had tried to make a nest in it.

Was this Cassandra's way of punishing his cousin for making demands on her time? Brandon wondered as everyone at the table began talking louder than necessary. Or was it a means of striking back at him for questioning her decision to reject his proposal?

If it was, then they could be snowbound at the Martins' farm for months without any hope of reconciling.

Chapter Eleven

Brandon Calvert was going to marry someone else. Cassandra kept reminding herself of that over and over as she changed clothes and carefully arranged her hair for the day. Each time it stung. But she continued to do it, hoping the exercise might inoculate her against the next time she must face him.

Not only was Brandon going to marry someone else, the lady in question would be far better suited to him than she could ever hope to be.

Imogene Calvert had taken great pains to sing Miss Reynolds' praises. "She is an heiress, you know. So neither of them will have any cause to suspect the other of fortune hunting."

Cassandra flinched. Of course Brandon's cousin could not know the deplorable state of her family's fortunes. But the fact that she had been travelling by public stagecoach rather than a private equipage must suggest she was no heiress.

Brandon might have a clearer impression of her situation, now that she had told him about her father's debts. Even if there were no other obstacles to a renewal of their courtship, he would surely be wary of making the same mistake his father had. How would he ever be able to trust that she could care for *him* rather than his money?

What difference did it make though? Cassandra stabbed a hair pin deep into a braided coil high on the back of her head. There were so many obstacles between them that another one scarcely mattered. Whether Brandon understood or not, refusing his proposal was one of the most prudent decisions she'd ever made. She would do it again if he were foolish enough to make her another offer.

Then what right did she have to object if he intended to wed another lady? Cassandra drew several slow, deep breaths and practiced a gracious smile. She would have given anything for a mirror to check whether her expression looked convincing.

She must stop dithering! If she stayed up here much longer it would look as if she was deliberately trying to avoid another encounter with Brandon. Cassandra refused to give him any grounds to suspect that.

Drawing confidence from her appearance, she marched downstairs with her head held high and her countenance serene. It remained that way until she spotted Sir Brandon Calvert standing at the foot of the stairs with his arms crossed. Cassandra's knees threatened to buckle and send her tumbling down the last few steps.

Pride saved her from landing at his feet in a pathetic heap.

She stopped and looked down at him. Then she swept a glance over the rest of the parlor and found it empty of guests, much to her relief. From the kitchen came the muted rattle of cutlery and a buzz of conversation.

"Did you wish to speak to me, Sir Brandon?" She strove to keep her voice cool and correct, unlike the way he'd last heard her speak. How pitiful she must have sounded.

He gave a curt nod. "You look very well, Lady Cassandra."

She should have been flattered, except that his compliment sounded more like an accusation.

"Why, thank you," she replied with wary civility. "Was there something else you wished to say? I cannot imagine you waited here simply to praise my appearance."

"Quite true." He stepped back to allow her to descend the rest of the stairs.

Cassandra would have preferred to stay looking down on him, but she could not ignore the pointed invitation.

          Deborah Hale

"Well?" She raised her eyebrows as she carefully descended. "Pray do not keep me in suspense."

How she wished his fierce scowl was not so compelling!

"You look very well," he repeated. "I wish I could say the same of my cousin. I am surprised and disappointed that you would vent your vexation with me upon a young person who looks up to you and has never done you any harm."

"You think I committed *that*?" Cassandra waved her hand wildly around her head to suggest Miss Calvert's efforts at hairdressing.

"Did you not?" The baronet's expression collapsed from grim severity into abject bewilderment so swiftly, the result was almost comical.

How could he believe her capable of committing such a grooming atrocity? Cassandra bridled. But Brandon's slack gape and the recollection of his cousin's scarecrow appearance made it nearly impossible to keep from laughing.

Somehow, she managed to master her mirth.

Shaking her head vigorously, she held up her hand, palm toward him. "On my honor, I had nothing to do with it."

Her assurance did not lessen his confusion. "But … you were going to help her get dressed."

"So I would have if she'd let me. I asked several times but she was determined to do it herself. Perhaps if you speak to her, she might reconsider."

"Why did she refuse your help?"

Though Cassandra had expected this question, it wiped the grin of amusement from her face. "Your cousin guessed that you and I once had a closer acquaintance than we admitted to. She accused me of breaking your heart. After that she wanted nothing more to do with me. I must say I admire her loyalty if not her hair."

Her quip provoked a faint grin from Brandon, but his expressive blue eyes held no hint of amusement.

With tension bristling between them, she had nothing to lose. The least she could gain from their remaining time together was the answers to some important questions. Those answers might help her truly make peace with the past.

"Was your cousin correct?" she demanded, knowing Brandon would have no choice but to answer truthfully. "Did I break your heart?"

His eyes widened as if she had shoved the barrel of a loaded pistol into his ribs. But after a moment's hesitation, he replied in a self-deprecating tone. "In the young, that organ is particularly fragile, but time is a great healer."

What had she hoped he would say? Cassandra scarcely knew. Of course she did not want the burden of knowing she had hurt him do deeply. Especially now that she'd begun to suspect her motives for rejecting him might not have been as unselfish as she'd once believed. Yet it pained her to hear him speak of his feelings in that off-hand manner, as if they had been nothing more than a youthful whim he'd outgrown.

Before she could decide how to reply, Brandon spoke again. "It seems I owe you an apology — more than one, in fact."

The abrupt shift in his manner caught her off-guard. "Do you? What for?"

"For suspecting you would deliberately make my cousin appear ridiculous." There could be no denying his sincerity. "I should have known you would never stoop to such vengeful behavior."

"So you should." Cassandra refused to let him off too easily. "But I accept your apology. I hope you will be able to accept mine."

Brandon's brow furrowed. Was it possible he did not know what she wanted to apologize for?

Just then, heavy footsteps and loud voices approached from the kitchen. The stagecoach driver and guard strode into the parlor.

Grateful as she was that they had found shelter in the Martins' snug cottage, at that moment Cassandra wished she and Brandon were the only inhabitants of a large mansion.

Perhaps then they could finish a conversation without being interrupted.

When they spied Cassandra and Brandon, the two men froze. "Pardon the intrusion Sir … and Miss. Now that the snow has stopped, we need to check the state of the roads to figure how soon we can be on our way again."

"No need to apologize." Cassandra moved out of their path so the men could reach the entry hall, where their coats and cloaks hung. "Do you suppose we shall get back on the road today?"

It would be better if she did not linger here, common sense informed her like a pedantic governess. She and Brandon had taken the opportunity to revisit the past and discuss her reasons for refusing his marriage proposal. Now he was on his way to propose to someone else, so there was nothing more to be said.

Nothing? Her heart rebelled. What about the fact that she still cared for him? For years she had tried to convince herself otherwise, but the past two days had shown her those feelings were not dead, only slumbering. The slightest encouragement had roused them awake again. Brandon's revelation about his family had made her feel she knew him better than ever. His experiences in the army had made him more mature and self-reliant, qualities she found potently attractive.

"I cannot swear to it, Miss." The coach driver's gravelly voice intruded upon Cassandra's thoughts. "But I hope we shall be able to get under way in the next few hours. With luck we should reach Bath before the day is out."

"I hope so," Cassandra heard herself reply, though her heart protested it was a lie. "My friend and I can be prepared to leave at a moment's notice whenever you are ready to go."

"Very good, Miss." The two men made their way past Cassandra and Brandon, their eyes politely averted as if they might be intruding on an intimate moment.

But that was ridiculous, of course.

"What about you, Sir Brandon?" Cassandra strove to keep

her tone crisp and impersonal. "You and your cousin must be anxious to join that house party we have heard so much about."

"Imogene will be eager to continue our journey as soon as possible, of course." Though Brandon did not refer to his own wishes, Cassandra assumed they must be the same as his cousin's. "But there is still the matter of our broken wheel. Even if the carriage can be dug out and a local blacksmith can repair it, I doubt we will be able to leave today. Besides, Mrs. Martin has invited us to stay for their Twelfth Night celebrations. After all her kindness, I cannot disappoint her."

"Twelfth Night, of course." Cassandra could imagine her great-aunt fuming if she and Mrs. Davis failed to arrive in time. By contrast, she pictured the Martins' kitchen table heaped with food while everyone talked and laughed as they feasted.

Even if Sir Brandon Calvert meant to marry someone else, Cassandra could not resist the desire for one more evening of his company — an evening untainted by silent recrimination or expectations. It would be an opportunity to replace the poignant memory of their last encounter with a more agreeable one that she would be happy to revisit in the years ahead.

Of all the days of Christmas, Twelfth Night was traditionally the merriest.

Brandon reflected on that while he and Cassandra made stilted conversation and the coach driver and guard donned their wraps to venture outside.

Twelfth Night was an occasion for feasting and exchanging gifts. It was a time for singing and dancing, for drinking punch and eating rich, lavishly decorated cakes. For as long as he could remember, his parents had hosted a grand ball on Twelfth Night, which was famed for its festivity.

For that one evening, the silent tension in their household had been replaced with music, conversation and laughter. His parents put on such a convincing show of domestic harmony that even he was tempted to believe it. Twelfth Night had been one day of the year when his parents appeared to love both their sons equally. Though he knew it was all a ruse for the benefit of their guests, Brandon had still enjoyed the celebration and look forward to it for the rest of the year.

If he could spend *this* Twelfth Night in the company of Lady Cassandra Whitney, Brandon reckoned it would eclipse all those past celebrations.

But did he deserve such a boon after the way he'd treated her?

All these years he'd thought ill of her, in a fruitless effort to purge her from his heart. Yet when she'd revealed her reason for refusing him, he had not even tried to understand her motives. Instead, he'd taken offence and lashed out at her. Then when Imogene appeared looking like a dog's breakfast, he had immediately concluded Cassandra must be to blame.

What made him so quick to suspect her of deceit and so reluctant to trust her? Could it be a tainted inheritance from his mother? If it was, could he make a conscious effort to change his attitude? Or would it always be warped, like wood exposed to the damp?

Brandon cast frequent disapproving glances at the coach driver and guard. Had they forgotten how to dress themselves? They were certainly taking their time about it. He feared Cassandra might remember some chore she must do for Mrs. Martin and rush away. To his relief, she lingered until the two men headed off.

When they threw open the door, an icy draft whipped down the hallway. Brandon shivered. The future seemed to skulk outside the Martins' cottage — cold, stark and empty — waiting to claim him.

The instant the door swung shut, he and Cassandra spoke at once.

"There is something I would like to say."

"One more thing, if I may?"

Their words clashed in the air making them both break off in thin, nervous laughter.

"Do go on," Cassandra bid him.

Brandon shook his head. "Ladies, first."

"Very well." She took a deep breath and squared her shoulders. "I owe you an apology. No doubt I owe you a great deal more than that, but it is all I have to offer."

"You have much more to offer." Brandon lowered his voice to a caressing murmur. What would he give for any of the delights that were in her power to bestow? At that moment he would have bartered everything he possessed for a single kiss. But would that be enough?

He hoped she might ask him to explain his cryptic remark, but she did not. Did she guess his meaning but shrink from hearing it in plainer language?

"Perhaps you are right," she continued as if he had not spoken. "Perhaps I should have told you of my father's intentions and allowed you to decide whether you still wished to marry me. If you had, I could still have refused your proposal, but at least you would have known the true reason why. You would have had no cause to think my decision reflected ill upon you — that you were somehow lacking. Nothing could have been further from the truth."

Cassandra's dark eyes flashed with passionate sincerity that called forth his old feelings for her.

Brandon shook his head. "You were trying to protect me from the most powerful source of misery you had ever encountered. You knew how contrary I could be. I might have insisted on going ahead with the marriage and it might have ruined me."

It galled him to admit the possibility, even if it was true.

"We can never know what might have happened," Cassandra replied. "But I deprived you of a choice you should have been given. At the time, I thought I was protecting you. In the years after, I repeated that excuse over and over until I made myself believe it. Now I fear my motives may have been more selfish than I wished to think."

"Selfish?" Brandon echoed in a doubtful tone. "In what way?"

Cassandra's whole being radiated reluctance to speak of it. "I wonder now if I was ashamed to expose the unsavory side of my father's character and my family's precarious circumstances. I wonder if my pride could not bear to have you reject me once you learned the truth."

They might not be noble motives, but they were ones with which Brandon could sympathize.

Her head bowed in shame, Cassandra glanced up at him through her fringe of black lashes. That look seemed to ask more than she could ever put into words. It made him long to plumb the depths of her mysterious dark gaze, so he could explore all her hidden feelings.

"You had good reason to be angry with me when I told you the truth at last," she murmured. "I told you before how much I regretted refusing you, but I regret misleading you even more. Can you ever forgive me for that?"

He reached out and gently clasped her hands. "My dearest Cassandra, there is nothing to forgive. At least, nothing on your part. I was unduly harsh with you earlier, when I ought to have been grateful — or at the very least understanding. My only defense is that your revelation took me by surprise. It made me imagine the life we might have had together if you'd told me the truth four years ago. The truth is you may have saved me from a different future than the one I foresaw."

The air between them seemed to shimmer as Brandon had sometimes seen it do on the hottest days of the Spanish summer. Unleashed, it might have the power to melt every flake of snow between here and Bath.

The last thing Brandon wanted was for that blessed snow to disappear. "I should have thanked you instead of judging and berating you. Is it too late to do that now or have I lost my chance?"

His pulse and breath both seemed to stop as he awaited Cassandra's answer.

"I want to believe there are always second chances," she replied in hesitant whisper.

She *wanted* to believe? That was a long way from certainty, but Brandon was willing to risk it. "In that case, thank you for trying to protect me four years ago. And thank you for telling me the truth today. I know it cannot have been easy."

"Then you do forgive me?" She sounded overwhelmed by the possibility.

Brandon felt overwhelmed too, by so many complicated emotions. "I thought that went without saying. But perhaps it does need to be said. Indeed, I do forgive you."

Speaking those words seemed to lift a heavy burden from his heart. He wished he had not held onto it for so long. "I beg *your* pardon for my earlier ingratitude."

The glow in Cassandra's eyes spoke volumes more than her breathless whisper. "Granted."

The brevity of her reply scarcely mattered when it came from such lips as hers. They reminded Brandon of ripe raspberries — full, soft and red. He reckoned they would be even sweeter to nibble. They seemed to call to his, making his lips tingle to kiss her.

But too many considerations held him back.

Good sense told him it was too soon. They had only just met again after a long separation and a parting fraught with ill feeling. Discretion warned that this was the wrong place. With so many people crammed into a small cottage, it was a wonder no one had intruded upon them in the past few minutes. The last thing he wanted was to compromise Cassandra's reputation and perhaps force them both into a situation for which they were not ready.

Brandon's sense of fairness weighed in too. Though he had made no formal commitment to Isabella Reynolds, he believed she guessed his intentions and would be expecting a proposal during the house party. He owed it to both ladies to end his connection with Miss Reynolds before kissing another woman. Last of all, but by no means least important, was the urgent whisper of caution. Cassandra might have rejected him for the kindest of reasons in the world, but it had devastated him nonetheless. Did he dare trust his heart to a woman who had proved herself capable of destroying it?

Chapter Twelve

W as Brandon going to kiss her? Cassandra sensed his intention like the invisible yet powerful pull of the moon upon the tides. She held herself in mute, quivering stillness, not wanting any sudden movement or word to break the spell that drew them toward one another.

At the same time, propriety demanded she must not do anything to encourage the affections of a man who intended to marry someone else. She told herself these were unique circumstances and she had a prior claim on the gentleman. Brandon had wanted her first. He would never have looked twice at that Miss Reynolds if Cassandra had accepted his proposal four years ago.

But she had not accepted, her conscience reminded her in the severest tone of her Great-aunt Augusta. That gave her no claim at all — less than none. Where would Society be if all the spurning sweethearts and jilting fiancées suddenly changed their fickle minds and set out to recapture the hearts of gentlemen they had rejected? Chaos!

Very well, she would do nothing to encourage him. But if Brandon tried to steal a kiss, as she sensed he might, no power on earth could persuade her to resist him.

The tension and anticipation between them intensified with each passing second. Just as that attraction became too potent for them to resist, a voice shattered it like a bauble of blown glass struck with a fire iron.

"There you are, Brandon." Imogene Calvert marched into the parlor with an air of regal authority at odds with her ridiculous appearance. "I wondered what could be detaining you. Now I see."

His cousin's sudden arrival roused Brandon as if from a sweet, improbable dream. He inhaled a sharp breath, sending a tremor through his tall, lean frame. He dropped Cassandra's hand with a guilty start. "What is it you want now, Imogene?"

"The same thing I have wanted for the past three days, of course." His cousin advanced upon them and insinuated herself between Brandon and Cassandra. "I want to get to Everleigh. Do not forget what awaits us there."

The young lady kept her back toward Cassandra as if she were unworthy of notice. Though Miss Calvert did not address a word to her, Cassandra recalled her last comment with harsh clarity.

"You may save your flattery and your flirtatious banter."

Did Brandon regard her behavior that way as well? Cassandra could hardly blame him after his family experience and her rejection. Though she'd only meant to spare him from being exploited by her father, her refusal had instead taught him that he could not trust others to have the feelings they claimed.

"I thought you must have gone out with the other men, to fetch someone to repair your carriage." Miss Calvert continued to address her cousin as if Cassandra was not even there. "Perhaps we will be able get back on the road today after all."

"I doubt it." Brandon replied. "Depending on how the snow has drifted, it could take hours to dig the carriage out."

"Then perhaps we should go in the stagecoach and leave Perkins to bring your carriage to Everleigh when it is ready. It may seem an odd arrangement, but I doubt the other guests will take exception to it under the circumstances."

Brandon hesitated. Cassandra held her breath. Would he agree to his cousin's suggestion or reject it? Did *she* want to share the stagecoach box with him all the way to Bath? They would not be alone, but at least it would allow her more time in his company. On the other hand, such a journey made it more likely he would discover the humble position she would occupy in her great-aunt's household.

She would have told him the truth about her circumstances if he had not been about to propose to another woman — an heiress at that. But if he was committed to someone else, what would it matter? It might only make Brandon suspect she was trying to snare him for his fortune. He had thought badly enough of her over the years. She could not bear to have him think worse now.

At last Brandon answered his cousin. "There is no guarantee the stagecoach will get on the road today, either. Besides, I promised Mrs. Martin we would celebrate Twelfth Night with them and I mean to keep my word."

Imogene Calvert stamped her foot like a petulant child denied her way. "What about your promise to take me to Everleigh? Does that count for nothing?"

"I mean to keep my promise to you," Brandon replied with admirable restraint. "But not necessarily today."

His cousin stormed and wheedled but he remained firm. "Are you certain you would want to appear at Everleigh looking as you do at the moment? Have you even glanced in a looking glass?"

Miss Calvert raised a hand to her hair as if she'd forgotten. "Is it that bad?"

"Worse." The flesh around Brandon's mouth flexed and tightened in an obvious effort to suppress a grin. "It is your own fault for never learning to look after yourself without the help of servants. And for refusing Lady Cassandra's generous offer of assistance."

"How could I accept?" Miss Calvert spun around to glare at Cassandra. "After the way she treated you, I would rather look a perfect fool than have such a person pretend to be kind to me."

"Then you have got your wish," Brandon rolled his eyes and pulled a droll face behind his cousin's back.

It was all Cassandra could do to contain the laughter that

bubbled up within her. It was not simply amusement at his antics, but relief that he seemed not to heed Miss Calvert's snide comment about her.

"Lady Cassandra has shown you sincere kindness," he continued, "perhaps more than you deserve."

"She has not!" With her wild tangle of hair and baleful glare, Imogene Calvert suddenly looked more sinister than comical. "She is only making a show of interest in me to appeal to you. Now that she has been on the shelf for a while she sees that you are a good catch after all. She is trying to win you back and I will not let her use me to do it!"

Those accusations skewered Cassandra's pride until it writhed, not least of all because there was a tiny grain of truth amid the condemnation.

"You are mistaken!" She struggled to suppress a furious blush which would make her appear guilty of all charges. "I was only trying to help you because it is what I hope others might do for my younger sisters if they were in your situation. I have no designs upon your cousin. I would never pursue a gentleman I had once refused!"

She expected Imogene Calvert to scoff, as her own conscience did. But something in her tone must have rung true enough to give Brandon's cousin second thoughts. "You wouldn't?"

Cassandra shook her head, even as she did battle with her conscience. She would have welcomed Brandon's attentions if he still had any feelings for her, but she would not make a fool of herself by pursuing him.

"Are you satisfied, Imogene?" her cousin demanded. "Lady Cassandra has no romantic interest in me whatsoever."

That was far from the truth, but Cassandra could not bring herself to contradict him.

"Not that it is any of your business," Brandon continued, all trace of levity gone. "Besides it is not necessary for you to prove your loyalty to me by being rude to Lady Cassandra. She and I are not enemies. I may not have been pleased when she declined my proposal but she had every right to exercise her choice. If her feelings for me were not sufficient to sustain a marriage between us, I am grateful to her for being truthful with me instead of allowing other considerations to influence her decision. That would not have been in the best interest of either of us."

He was right, of course, about several of the things he'd said. Cassandra could not deny it. And yet, it grieved her to hear him speak of her refusal as if it had turned out to be a fortunate escape.

Brandon clasped his hands behind his back and regarded Miss Calvert with the air of a stern father rather than a cousin. "Now, I believe you owe Lady Cassandra an apology."

The young lady hesitated for a long moment then turned and dropped a curtsey to Cassandra. "I beg your pardon for anything I said that was not true. I sincerely hope you can excuse me, for my cousin's sake."

She did not sound entirely sincere in her apology. Her wording seemed suspicious, for one thing. Cassandra wondered if the young lady blamed her for Brandon's annoyance. Yet, for his sake, she was prepared to bear with his cousin, no matter how disagreeable the girl might be to her.

"There is no need for an apology, Sir Brandon. I understand why your cousin would not wish to consort with anyone she believed had injured you. I would do no less in her place. All I ask is for her to accept my assurance that I have no designs upon you, though I do wish you all the good fortune and happiness in the world."

"Of course," Miss Calvert murmured, though Cassandra sensed she was not convinced.

Which part did she doubt — Cassandra's assertion that she wished Brandon well or her denial of any romantic interest in him? Imogene Calvert might not be the most sensible person, but she was no fool.

Cassandra sensed it would take more than a lecture from Brandon to make his cousin view her as anything but a threat.

It appeared his cousin had saved him from making a colossal fool of himself, Brandon reflected as Cassandra and Imogene returned upstairs to repair his cousin's toilette.

If she had not intruded when she did, he would certainly have succumbed to the temptation to kiss Cassandra. If she had not flung about ridiculous accusations, he would not have heard from Cassandra's own lips that she had no romantic feelings for him.

Clearly the response he'd sensed from her had been nothing but remorse, perhaps with a flicker of their old camaraderie. He must put Lady Cassandra Whitney out of his mind once and for all. He must return to his sensible plan to secure Miss Reynolds. At least now that he had confronted Cassandra, the old, festering wound to his heart had been lanced so it could heal properly.

Now that he knew the truth about her feelings, he need not linger around the cottage and risk falling prey to any more foolish fancies about a lady who wanted nothing more to do with him.

He strode off to the kitchen and summoned his driver and footman. They both seemed quite comfortable. Perkins was drinking tea while Edward cracked nuts into a bowl for Mrs. Martin.

"Why do we need to go out, sir?" the young footman asked, clearly not eager to stir outside on a winter morning. "I thought we were going to stay here another night."

"We are." Brandon tried not to vent his romantic frustration on his servant. "But we still need to make preparations so we can get back on the road tomorrow. Otherwise I fear we may suffer my cousin's wrath."

Perkins gave an indulgent chuckle. "Miss Calvert is a spirited young lady."

Edward rose from the table. "If you will excuse me, Mrs. Martin, I have most of the nuts cracked for you."

Their hostess glanced toward the bowl he held out for her inspection. "That's a great help, thank you. Truth to tell,

I would just as soon have you men go about your business so we women can make preparations for this evening."

With that, the three men bundled up and headed off to the village. The sky was still overcast but the wind had died down and the air was a good deal milder. In some places the road had been blown free of snow, which drifted deeply elsewhere.

"At least we can see where we are going, today," said Brandon. "No chance of losing our way and wandering onto the downs."

"That's true, sir." Perkins pointed to a cluster of buildings ahead. "If we'd only known how near the village was, we might have pressed on the other night."

Would it have been better if they had reached Cherhill and put up at the inn? Brandon wondered. Then he would not have been forced into such close contact with Cassandra. They might not have had an opportunity to talk over the past and make peace with it.

Brandon spied several villagers making paths through the snow, the way he had done to the Martins' well. Some of the men were taking the opportunity to amuse their children at the same time, by towing them on the boards instead of rocks to compact the snow. As he listened to the youngster's laughter and sensed their warm family connection, a pang of envy smote him. No doubt the villagers worked harder than he'd ever been obliged to, with fewer comforts to show for it. But his experience and Cassandra's proved that rank and fortune did not insure happiness.

She had denied her feelings for Brandon a second time. That was the kind of falsehood he rightly despised. Cassandra's conscience reproached her as she worked to make Imogene Calvert look presentable.

"Your buttons are not hooked quite properly at the back." Cassandra set about fixing the problem. "It is difficult for a lady to manage on her own."

She found herself talking more than usual to smooth the

awkwardness of Miss Calvert's sullen silence. It was clear the young lady had not been entirely reassured by what she and Brandon had to say about their past acquaintance. Not only did his cousin still seem to blame Cassandra for hurting him with her rejection. Miss Calvert also seemed to view her as some sort of threat.

"That looks better." She strove to conceal her annoyance with Brandon's cousin for shattering her lovely moment with him. She would have left the ungrateful girl to her own devices, but she looked on this as a sort of penance for her behavior. "Now let's see what we can do about your hair."

"I suppose you regret the way you treated my cousin." Miss Calvert broke her silence to echo Cassandra's very thoughts. "No one ever told me your name, but Mama did mention that he was badly treated and wanted nothing to do with women or marriage for quite some time afterwards."

Cassandra tried not to flinch from the charge. Instead she focused her attention on combing out the golden tangle of Miss Calvert's hair. "I expect many people have made mistakes in their youth which they regret later. I am pleased to hear your cousin has come to view my past actions in a positive light."

"Yes, that was very sensible of him. He must realize that if you'd accepted him, he would not have had the opportunity to marry Miss Reynolds. Ouch! Must you pull so hard with that comb?"

"I beg your pardon." Cassandra willed herself to use an even lighter touch, but it was not easy. "I am trying to be as gentle as I can. Perhaps if you had let me comb it out earlier . . ."

Was Imogene Calvert right? Had Brandon been able to forgive her because her refusal left him free to pursue a better match? If that were true, why had he never mentioned Miss Reynolds or his intention of proposing to her?

None of that mattered now, Cassandra reminded herself with considerable severity. She would be on her way to Bath before the day was out. There was a good chance she would not even see Brandon before she left. Now that she'd had told him the truth about her past actions and discovered it made no difference, perhaps she could finally put the whole matter behind her, where it belonged. She could begin to make a somewhat independent life for herself and do her best to assist her sisters and Letty.

Now that Miss Calvert had found her voice again, she insisted on extolling the merits of Miss Reynolds, who sounded like a perfect paragon. "She is vastly accomplished, you know. She sings divinely while accompanying herself on the pianoforte."

"Indeed?" Cassandra's cheeks ached from the effort to keep smiling.

"She paints perfectly splendid watercolors," Miss Calvert gushed. "And she dances like an angel!"

When had Miss Calvert seen an angel dance to be able to draw that comparison? Cassandra struggled to suppress the question for it might suggest she had not been entirely truthful earlier.

"Miss Reynolds is very handsome as well." Imogene Calvert continued with fiendish delight, as if she sensed every word of praise for Brandon's future wife was like a sharp pin poked into Cassandra. "Her hair is the color of honey and her eyes are the very same shade of blue as Brandon's."

It took a great effort of will for Cassandra to unclench her teeth. "They should make a fine-looking couple."

Privately she wondered how a lady with so many fine qualities and a large fortune had managed to remain single for more than a year after making her debut.

Before Miss Calvert could find more to praise about Isabella Reynolds, Cassandra forestalled her. "Now that your hair is done, you must excuse me. I believe Mrs. Martin can use my help to prepare for this evening."

"Of course." Imogene Calvert turned to regard Cassandra with an infuriating little smirk. "Though I'm sure Miss Reynolds would never think of stooping to do chores for a farmer's wife."

Cassandra refused to let the insult provoke her. "Then it is fortunate for Miss Reynolds that she was not snowbound with us. I do not consider it *beneath* me to assist others, no matter what their station in life."

That sounded very virtuous, her conscience chided as she strode away. But what about *accepting* help from others? That was something her pride found harder to tolerate.

Chapter Thirteen

ONCE BRANDON LOCATED the Cherhill blacksmith and explained the problem with his disabled carriage, it required several hours work for the necessary repairs to be completed.

When Perkins brought the horses to haul the vehicle back to the Martin farm, Brandon surveyed the lengthening shadows. "Just as I expected. Even with ideal roads, I doubt we could have reached Bath before dark."

The roads were far from ideal, if the stretch between here and Cherhill was any indication.

"I don't mind staying another night, sir." Edward stamped his feet to warm them. "I look forward to a tasty meal at Mrs. Martin's table and plenty of good cheer."

"So do I," Brandon replied. "Let us not delay another moment getting back there."

No doubt the festivities would prove very pleasant. But they would not be the same without Cassandra. Like an unexpected blow, Brandon suddenly realized he had not bid her farewell. Stung by her insistence that she no longer had any romantic interest in him, he'd been relieved to escape her presence. He had not wanted to risk his tone or manner betraying his bitter disappointment.

By now the stagecoach must have left for Bath, whisking her out of his life again. He hoped she would have a safe journey. Would she and Mrs. Davis reach their destination before dark? He did not like to think of her being stranded again without him.

But when they reached the Martins' barnyard, he spied the unharnessed stagecoach parked there. Clearly the coachman must have had second thoughts about the wisdom of pressing on with their journey today. Or perhaps the prospect of celebrating Twelfth Night at the Martins' farm had tempted him to linger. Whatever the reason, Brandon wanted to shake his hand.

Perhaps there was no hope for Cassandra and him to regain what they'd lost. But at least now he could say a proper farewell, wish her Godspeed and part as friends.

"There you are." Mr. Martin emerged from the barn as they led the horses toward it. "I was afraid you might need a team of oxen to pull your carriage out of the snow. As you can see, our party is not breaking up quite yet."

While his servants stabled the horses, Brandon lingered in the barn, anxious for a private word with Tobias Martin.

"What are you still doing out here?" asked the farmer when Brandon stayed behind after his driver and footman had retired to the house. "I thought you'd want to be inside making up to Lady Cassandra, not out here in the cold with me and the livestock. I reckon she'd prefer it as well."

Brandon knew he should not respond to the remark, but carry on with what he intended to say. But somehow he could not resist the opportunity to talk about Cassandra — even if it was only to deny anything between them. "I reckon she would be just as happy if I stayed out here all evening."

He prepared to return to the matter he'd intended to discuss but Mr. Martin seemed to find his statement too provocative to ignore. "What makes you certain of that? Is it the way her face lights up when the two of you talk together? Or is it the way she watches you when you're not looking? You may not have noticed, but I have."

Brandon shook his head. Tempting as it was to believe the farmer, he had been tantalized by hope too often during the past forty-eight hours only to be disappointed. "You are mistaken, I fear."

He sensed Mr. Martin would not stop his well-intentioned meddling until he understood why a match between his two guests was quite impossible. "Lady Cassandra and I have a prior acquaintance, you see."

"So I've heard." The farmer glanced toward the cottage. "I gather you once asked the lady to wed and she turned you down."

"Where did you hear that?" Brandon demanded.

Tobias Martin shrugged. "From my wife, who had it from the lady herself. Now I daresay it was a bitter disappointment. A fine-looking gentleman like you with a comfortable fortune wouldn't expect to be refused. But did no one ever teach you the importance of persistence?"

"I appreciate your concern," Brandon could not suppress a sigh. "But I fear you do not understand my situation."

"Don't I, though?" Mr. Martin gave an indulgent chuckle. "Do you suppose my missus snapped me up the first time I asked? Her father was the village butcher with a good business and a bit put by. And Effie was the prettiest, liveliest lass in the parish. The cooper and the innkeeper's son were both mad for her."

It made Brandon smile to picture the hardy farmer as an ardent young swain and his motherly wife as the belle of rural Wiltshire. "But you prevailed against such competition. I congratulate you. How did you manage it?"

Mr. Martin's broad chest puffed up larger still. "With constancy and tenacity. The others stopped asking after she refused them once. But I kept asking didn't I? I showed her my feelings were more than a flash in the pan but would wear well over the years."

If only his parents could have had that kind of marriage, Brandon reflected, how many lives might have been better for it?

"I commend you, sir, but I fear my situation is not the same. Lady Cassandra told me plainly that she no longer has any romantic feelings for me."

Mr. Martin shook his head slowly. "That is not what she told my wife."

Brandon ruthlessly quelled another rogue flicker of hope that leapt within him. Would he never learn? "Don't you think it is possible Mrs. Martin misunderstood or heard what she wanted to?"

"That could be." The farmer did not sound convinced. "But I reckon it's just as likely the lady might be reluctant to confess her feelings for a gentleman she believed was lost to her, after she'd once refused him."

Their host's suggestion had a ring of truth that Brandon found very difficult to dismiss. After all, had he not been reluctant to confess that he still cared for a woman who had refused him once?

"Have you really got so much to lose by trying again?" the farmer asked. "Those other men thought they did after Effie turned them down, but I believed there was more to gain. I cannot tell you what to do, but I hope you'll consider what I've said. Now we had better get inside before Effie sends a search party after us."

Did he have so much to lose? Brandon wondered. More than Mr. Martin might realize. His pride, for a start, and perhaps the opportunity to make a safe, sensible union with Isabella Reynolds. But did those possible losses weigh anything compared to what he might gain?

How would Brandon react when he learned that the stagecoach party would be staying another night at the Martins' farm?

As she stirred up the parlor fire, Cassandra kept her ears open for the baronet's voice or footfall in the entryway.

Would he resent having to spend another evening in her company when he would rather be with the incomparable Miss Reynolds? Or would he welcome the opportunity to bring matters between them to a satisfactory conclusion?

When the stagecoach driver had informed Cassandra that

the roads were not yet fit for travelling, a surge of elation had risen in her heart. It was tempered with a qualm of guilt, as if she'd received an expensive gift she did not deserve. That gift was the opportunity to enjoy one last evening with Brandon and say a proper goodbye.

The front door opened and closed, followed by muted voices and the rustle of coats being removed. Cassandra's heart began to race and her cheeks blazed with heat that did not come from the low fire.

A moment later, Sir Brandon's coachman and footman entered the parlor. Their faces were nipped red from the cold.

"Where has my cousin got to?" demanded Imogene Calvert, who sat by the hearth, studiously ignoring Cassandra. "He is the one who insisted we must stay here another night."

"The master should be along in a moment, Miss," the footman replied. "He was having a word with Mr. Martin when we came in."

Rising from the hearth Cassandra dusted off her hands as she turned toward the two men. "If you would care for a hot drink, Mrs. Martin has cider in the kitchen."

Both men smiled at the prospect of hot cider.

"What about you, Miss?" the footman asked Imogene Calvert. "Shall I fetch you a cup?"

"That is kind of you to offer, Edward." The young lady cast a sidelong glance at Cassandra, perhaps considering whether she wanted to remain in the same room with her. "A hot drink would be very pleasant. I believe I will join you and the others in the kitchen."

Once they were gone, Cassandra took the opportunity to tidy the now-empty parlor. Just as she was finishing, she heard someone else enter through the front door. She peeked into the entry hall to find Brandon removing his greatcoat.

Before she could step away, he spotted her and broke into an unexpected smile. "Lady Cassandra. Just the person I wanted to see. I understand your party will be staying on tonight after all. A wise decision by your driver, in my opinion."

He beckoned her toward him, an invitation Cassandra could not resist. It seemed he was prepared to be more than civil to her during this final evening they must spend together. Perhaps it was because of what he'd told his cousin— he realized the positive effect her rejection had on his life. Whatever the reason, she would be grateful if it made their last hours together reasonably congenial.

"Of course you believe it is a wise decision, since it happens to agree with yours." She teased him, to show that she was willing to be cordial if he was. "Mrs. Martin seems pleased, bless her hospitable heart. Most people would be relieved to entertain half as many unexpected house guests."

Brandon nodded. "That is what I wished to discuss with you ... at least something related. I want to compensate these good people for the invaluable service they have done us. But when I offered Mr. Martin a sum of money just now, he got quite vexed with me, as if I had insulted him. I do not know what to make of it. I hoped you might be able to enlighten me. You always seemed to have a better grasp of human nature than I."

His praise kindled a soft glow inside Cassandra, even though she knew he meant nothing by it. "I doubt that is true, but I believe I may understand why Mr. Martin took exception to your generous offer."

Would Brandon suggest they go into the parlor and discuss the matter? Cassandra preferred to linger in the narrow entryway. There was something informal — even intimate — about it.

"Do not keep me in suspense," Brandon's blue eyes shimmered ... with curiosity, no doubt.

"This may not be easy for a baronet to understand," she began. "In spite of his humbler station — indeed because of it — I suspect Mr. Martin is a proud man at heart."

"Proud?" Brandon's lofty brow furrowed and his wide mouth settled into a doubtful frown.

"I do not mean in the sense of haughty or superior,"

Cassandra explained. She was all too familiar with that sort of pride. "More self-respecting."

Why did it matter so much to her that Brandon grasp her explanation? Could it be because she was describing her own character as much as their host's?

Brandon could sympathize with the sort of pride Cassandra had described. He lifted silent thanks to whatever kind Providence had provided him with this excuse to reach out to her. He also welcomed the good fortune of finding her alone in the parlor. He must make the most of this unexpected opportunity.

"I believe I see what you are saying." He relished the chance to converse with her on any subject. "But what does that have to do with Mr. Martin's refusal to accept my money? The sum I offered is nothing to me, but the assistance we received in our hour of need was priceless."

He was especially grateful for the opportunity to become reacquainted with Cassandra in a home blessed by love — something neither of them had experienced when growing up. It had shown him what might be possible, not only in romantic fancies but in the very real world of a small Wiltshire farm.

"I quite agree." The warmth in Cassandra's voice suggested she approved of his thoughts as well as his words. "But I believe Mr. Martin has found it most agreeable to have a baronet and a duke's daughter as guests in his home. To accept payment from us would make him seem no better than an innkeeper. But to host a party like ours, puts him on an equal footing with any of us."

"I believe I see what you mean," Brandon ventured. "It would be as if the Prince Regent came to visit at *my* house. It would be an honor to host a royal guest, but I would feel my hospitality was cheapened if he offered to pay for it."

"You *do* understand!" cried Cassandra.

His insight seemed to gratify her beyond anything he'd

expected. Her lips spread into a disarming grin that made him yearn to imbibe of her high spirits with a kiss. If only he could be as certain of *her* feelings as Mr. Martin claimed to be.

"There is one difference," she added.

"And what might that be?" Brandon dropped his voice to a fond, bantering murmur. He would gladly spend the next several hours standing in this cramped, shadowy passageway that reeked of damp wool. As long as Cassandra was there to look upon and laugh with, no fashionable assembly hall or elegant country house could equal it.

"Merely that His Royal Highness would never think of insulting anyone by offering to pay." She tossed her head, daring him to reproach her impudence. "To be fair, the prince is generally quick to offer his hospitality in return, often on a lavish scale."

"That is it — the ideal solution!" In his elation, Brandon seized her hand. Or perhaps he had only been looking for an excuse. "I knew I was right to consult you."

"I am pleased you think so." Cassandra's smile flickered on and off, like a candle flame in a breeze. "But I am not certain what problem you are referring to, let alone what solution you believe I suggested."

Was she wavering between the propriety of pulling her hand away and the desire to leave it where it was? Brandon could not fault her indecision. He had felt similarly torn many times, with caution or conscience urging him one way while his heart tugged him in the other.

"You shall see." He gave her hand a squeeze, hoping it would not push her away. "Mr. Martin should be coming in any moment now and I mean to follow your guidance."

"You intrigue me." A suggestion of laughter bubbled beneath her words. "I suppose I must stay to appease my curiosity."

The sparkle in her dark eyes assured Brandon she was not sorry to have an excuse to linger in his company.

True to his prediction, they soon heard the farmer outside,

stamping the snow off his boots. With a pang of reluctance, Brandon released Cassandra's hand.

When Tobias Martin entered, he gave a little start at the sight of them. "What is this, a welcoming party?"

He removed his tricorne hat and unwound the long knitted muffler from around his neck.

Brandon was relieved that he sounded in better spirits than when they had spoken earlier, "You might say it is an *apologizing party*, sir, though Lady Cassandra is only here for moral support."

Their host shook his head as he hung up his outer garments. "I'm afraid none of that made a particle of sense to me."

"Then I shall be plain," said Brandon. "I want to beg your pardon for offering payment in exchange for your generous hospitality. No disrespect was intended, I assure you — quite the contrary. I realize no sum I could offer would begin to repay the debt we owe you and your good wife. You may well have saved seven lives."

"Hardly. You would soon have reached the village. Besides, any honest folk would have been moved to assist stranded travelers." In spite of his protests, Mr. Martin looked secretly pleased.

"I am obliged to you beyond any means of repayment," Brandon continued, "but I would be honored if you and Mrs. Martin would come to London as my guests, when the weather is better for travelling."

"That is a most handsome invitation and the honor would be ours." The farmer sounded flustered, but pleasantly so.

Brandon cast a fleeting glance at Cassandra. The radiance of her smile set his spirits soaring.

"Mother will be tickled when I tell her," Mr. Martin continued. "But with the farm … the stock … it is not easy to get away."

Brandon waved away his objections. "Surely we can find someone trustworthy to run the place in your absence for a few days. You and your good wife deserve a holiday."

"Indeed you do!" Cassandra chimed in. "I shall be happy to come and look after the house while you are away. Think how much it would mean to your wife."

Much as Brandon appreciated her support, he hoped Cassandra might play a different role in the Martins' visit.

"We shall see," the farmer replied. "Who knows what the future may bring? Having you here has not be an imposition, truly. Mother and I have enjoyed your company. Now, I smell roast goose. Let us go through and find out what Mother has for us to eat."

They did as Mr. Martin proposed and found the kitchen a beehive of industry. Everyone was talking and laughing together as they completed a variety of small tasks for the lady of the house. Even Imogene had abandoned her usual airs and graces. She stirred some kind of batter in a bowl while chatting quite amiably with Edward, who sat beside her peeling potatoes.

Cassandra approached Mrs. Martin, who stood by the hearth watching a number of pots suspended from hooks over the fire. "Forgive me. I did not mean to abandon you. What can I do?"

"And I," Brandon added. "I cannot sit idle while everyone else is busy."

Their hostess swept a glance around the kitchen. "The preparations for dinner are well in hand. To tell the truth, I fear you would only be under foot out here. You could go into the parlor and push the chairs out of the way, so we can dance later."

"Dance?" Brandon tried to imagine how they would manage that feat in such a small space. He associated dancing with large numbers of people in vast ballrooms and assembly halls.

Their hostess clearly had other ideas. She planted her hands on her ample hips. "That's what I said. You've heard of dancing, I trust? How are we to have a proper celebration of Twelfth Night without it? Now off you go. Once you finish, you can come back and set the table."

Was Mrs. Martin deliberately arranging matters so he and Cassandra would be off by themselves, away from the rest of the party? Brandon wondered as they marched away. He would not put it past their hostess. From the moment they'd arrived, Mrs. Martin had seemed eager to push them together. How far would she go to promote a match between them? He doubted she would lie, especially not to her husband. But might she shade the truth a little or interpret things she'd been told in a way she wanted to believe?

He turned toward Cassandra and pulled a wry face. "I have not been ordered about in that fashion since I resigned my commission. It was all I could do to keep from saluting her."

Cassandra pressed her lips together but laughter sputtered out in spite of her efforts. Nothing else he'd done recently had brought Brandon as satisfying a sense of accomplishment as making her smile and laugh.

With a sweep of his hand, he indicated the Martin's parlor. "Do *you* think there is space enough here to dance properly?'

"I expect we shall find out soon." Cassandra grasped one arm of a heavy wooden chair and tugged. It scarcely budged.

Brandon seized the other side and together they dragged it to the back wall. Three others followed.

"Where shall we put that one?" Brandon nodded toward the remaining chair.

"Will it fit in the entry hall?" Cassandra dusted off her hands. "I doubt anyone will be going in or out this evening."

They soon discovered it did fit, with an inch to spare on either side.

"Dear me!" cried Cassandra, who had pulled the chair back into place while Brandon pushed. "I seem to have boxed myself in. I shall have to climb over. Do not look, I beg you, for it will be most ungraceful."

"I do not believe you are capable of ungraceful movement." Brandon braced his knees on the seat of the chair and held his arms out to her. "Come, I can lift you over."

For an instant Cassandra looked as if she meant to refuse,

but then she stepped forward, placing her arms on his shoulders while his hands circled her slender waist. "Mind you do not lift me too high and dash my brains out on that ceiling beam."

"Never fear," Brandon gave a rather breathless chuckle. "I will not let any harm come to you."

That seemed to be all the reassurance Cassandra needed, for she launched herself toward him and Brandon hoisted her over the chair. He took great care not to set her back on her feet too abruptly for fear she might lose her balance. Instead he held her as long as she needed to get her proper footing ... and perhaps a trifle longer.

Her nearness made him feel as if *he* had struck his head on the thick ceiling beam — befuddled and not fully in control of himself. Instead of the pain such a blow should have inflicted, he was overcome by a jolt of pleasure.

He could not bring himself to let Cassandra go just yet. "Perhaps there is room enough here for dancing after all. Shall we try?"

"If you like."

He relinquished his grip on her waist to clasp her hands in his. Then he led her in a sidelong sashay, the width of the room and back to the center. There he twirled her around.

"I believe it will do nicely." Indeed, he now suspected the Martins' parlor would make a much pleasanter venue for dancing than any assembly or ballroom he'd ever frequented. "I hope you will do me the honor of at least one dance this evening."

"I can safely promise you that, Sir Brandon." Gently she disengaged her hands from his and sank into a charming curtsey. "In a company of this size, it would appear most unfriendly if we went the whole evening without dancing once together."

Brandon returned her curtsey with a gallant bow. "That would never do, would it? Now that we have talked things over and cleared the air, I hope we can be good friends again as we used to be."

They used to be more than friends and that was what he wished to recapture. For now he could be content to count her as his friend and build upon that firm foundation.

"Friends, of course." Cassandra glanced up at him in a manner that sent Brandon's heart into a wild, joyful dance of his own.

Yet when he gazed into her wide, dark eyes, he glimpsed a trace of secret sorrow in their depths, bewildering and unfathomable. His first instinct was to wonder if Cassandra might be hiding something more from him, but he pushed the thought roughly from his mind. If he was to have any hope of winning her again, he must learn to do one of the hardest things he could imagine … trust her.

Chapter Fourteen

FRIENDSHIP, OF COURSE.

Cassandra willed her smile not to falter even as her spirits deflated. How foolish of her to think Sir Brandon Calvert could want anything more from her. He might have been generous enough to forgive her abominable treatment of him. But she could not expect him to trust her with his heart again. She had broken it once already, like a clumsy housemaid handling the best china.

He had found a lady who would take better care of it — one who could have no secret motives for wanting to marry him. Tomorrow morning he would drive away to propose to Miss Reynolds, confident that she would accept his offer and treat it as the honor it was.

In the meantime, Brandon's request to dance with her was nothing more than courtesy. Any flirtation she'd sensed between them was on her side alone. The kiss she'd believed he meant to give her was only her wish, not his. She must not trick herself into believing otherwise.

Cassandra took a step back to put a more decorous distance between them. "Now that you are satisfied the Martins' parlor is large enough for dancing, I believe there is a table that needs to be set for our Twelfth Night dinner."

As she started toward the kitchen, she assured herself Brandon's friendship was precisely what she wanted. Even if he could recover from her past rejection sufficiently to care for her again, a match between them was no more advisable than it had been four years ago.

Her father was no longer around, threatening to leech Brandon's fortune. But would she be any better? How could she bear to live in luxury with a wealthy husband while Letty and her sisters were forced to practice strictest economy while residing in virtual charity on Lord Highworth's estate? Yet how could she expect any man she married to assist her family as she wished to?

Any man with a comfortable fortune who married her could never be certain she had wed him for love alone. With Brandon Calvert in particular, it would be like the worst of their parents' doomed marriages. He deserved better than that.

"There you are!" cried Mrs. Martin when Cassandra and Brandon entered the crowded kitchen. "I was afraid you'd forgotten us."

Her words might have sounded like a scolding but her tone was infused with warm approval.

Cassandra hoped she had not given their hostess an excuse to try her hand at matchmaking.

"The food will be ready soon." The farmer's wife stirred a bubbling pot of gravy that gave off the most delectable aroma. "Tobias, my dear, could I trouble you to pour my helpers some punch. You may all enjoy it at your leisure in the parlor while the table gets set."

Her husband and guests were quick to follow Mrs. Martin's orders, even Miss Calvert, who seemed in better spirits than she'd been all day. Once the others had retired to the parlor with their drinks, Brandon and Cassandra spread a linen cloth over the kitchen table then began setting places with all the plates and cutlery they could find in the old sideboard.

"I must go wash my face and put on a clean apron," Mrs. Martin announced. "If you smell anything burning, take it off the fire and give it a stir."

As their hostess bustled away, Cassandra cast a fleeting glance at Brandon, only to find him staring back with a gleeful grin. "Considering the modest size of this cottage and the number of people presently occupying it, you and I spend a surprising amount of time alone."

The playful pitch of his voice and the endearing crinkles of mirth around his eyes provoked a bubbly, tickling sensation deep inside Cassandra. It urged her to abandon all pride and propriety, giving no thought to the future. It required all her willpower to resist its siren song.

"Perhaps everyone else in the party secretly detests our society," she teased him, as she had once so enjoyed doing. "Perhaps they are happy to be rid of us for a time, even if we are only as far away as another room."

Brandon pretended to give the idea serious consideration as he set the cutlery beside each plate. "They might feel that way about me. But you? I cannot believe it. No one could be held in such universal esteem. From the beginning of this whole misadventure, you have been unfailingly helpful and good-natured. I would not have thought it possible, but the past four years seem to have improved you."

His words touched Cassandra, even more because she knew it was not the fatuous flattery of a beau but the honest praise of a friend. "You are kind to say so and I hope you are right. There was plenty of room for improvement in my character and still is, I daresay. Besides, not *everyone* is as tolerant of my faults as you seem to be."

A brief spasm of confusion crossed his features. "Imogene, you mean? I thought I set her straight, the little wretch. Has she been rude to you again? Has she made any more ridiculous accusations?"

He slammed down the final knife with such force that it made the rest of the cutlery on the table jump. His indignation seemed excessive for one friend defending another, but surely that was all it could be.

"Your cousin has been perfectly polite," Cassandra assured him, "though I am not certain she trusts me. There, the table is set and I do not smell anything burning. I hope Mrs. Martin will be satisfied with our stewardship of her kitchen, however brief."

"Indeed I am!" Their hostess bustled in, followed by her husband and the other guests. "Now find a seat, everyone and let us eat while the food is hot."

As the rest of the party squeezed in around the table and Mr. Martin sharpened his carving knife, Cassandra carried steaming bowls of vegetables to add to the feast.

Once their host's knife was sharpened to his satisfaction and his wife brought the brimming gravy boat, Mr. Martin swept a benevolent glance around the crowded table. "Before we tuck in, let us not forget to give thanks. Sir Brandon, would you do us the honor of saying grace?"

"The honor will be mine." Brandon rose and bowed his head while Mrs. Martin gave Cassandra a nudge toward the empty seat beside him. "Oh Lord, we give thanks for your bounty. Not only what we are about to partake from this table, but also for the kindness we have found in the hearts of those around it. Amen."

The others echoed the word, endorsing Sir Brandon's sentiment — none with greater conviction than Cassandra. Initially, she had not viewed this unexpected meeting with her former suitor as a blessing — quite the contrary. But she had come to appreciate it more with each passing hour.

The next little while passed in a pleasant blur of eating and drinking, talking and laughing. Cassandra could not recall when she had enjoyed a meal more. The goose was moist and flavorful, the gravy smooth and savory. Even the turnip and sprouts — neither of which were her favorites — tasted quite delicious this evening. But that feast for the palate scarcely compared to the one for her other senses. Seated beside Brandon, she savored frequent glances at his fine profile. He had not shaved properly since their arrival. Now the dark bristle of whiskers on his lower face lent his features a provocative roguish air.

As they reached for something on the crowded table, Brandon's arm brushed against hers. That brief contact sent a surge of sweet, tingling energy through her. It made her forget that tomorrow they must go their separate ways, she to a life of spinster servitude with her great-aunt, he to propose to another woman. Until then, nothing must taint her enjoyment of this evening and his delightful company.

"I hope you have left room for the cake," said Mrs. Martin as she rose and fetched it. "It may not be decorated as fancy as those in the pastry-cook's window in town, but I hope the flavor will make up for it."

She began serving out thick slices.

Brandon passed a piece to Cassandra. "If your cake tastes half as good as it smells, my dear Mrs. Martin, we shall all have another blessing for which to be thankful."

Their hostess beamed with pleasure as everyone tasted the cake and pronounced it delicious. "Watch for the bean and the pea that I baked into it. Whoever gets them shall be king and queen for the rest of the evening and must lead off the dancing."

Cassandra recalled that tradition surrounding the Twelfth Night cake. She bit into her slice with care, hoping fortune might favor her and Brandon with the roles of king and queen.

"I found the pea!" Imogene Calvert squealed like a child, her earlier airs forgotten.

"I have the bean!" Brandon's young footman held it out to show the others, as if he doubted they would believe him.

Everyone congratulated the pair and Brandon proposed a royal toast. Cassandra wondered if his cousin would take offense at being cast as the consort of a humble footman, but Miss Calvert did not seem to mind in the least.

"Now it is time to retire to the parlor," said Mr. Martin, "with Your Majesties' kind permission, of course. While our dinner settles, we shall each entertain you with a song, a story or a recitation."

Miss Calvert and the footman conferred then declared themselves pleased with the idea.

"Shall I help you clear away, Mrs. Martin?" Cassandra asked.

The farmer's wife shook her head. "There will be plenty

of time for that later, my dear. Now we must take our ease and enjoy ourselves."

As the king and queen led the procession back to the parlor, Cassandra found herself bringing up the rear with Brandon.

"What will you perform for your party piece?" He caught her hand and gave it a playful squeeze that made her heart skip several beats. "Will you favor us with a song, perhaps?"

"I fear I must." She dared to press his hand in return, assuring herself it was only a friendly gesture. "Mr. and Mrs. Martin do not have a pianoforte I can play and I have not the least knack for telling stories or reciting. What should I sing?"

Ahead of them she could hear a humorous ceremony to seat Miss Calvert and the footman in places of honor. Meanwhile, the rest of the party remained bottled up in the passageway to the kitchen. Much as she looked forward to dancing, Cassandra did not mind lingering behind the others with Brandon.

In response to her question, he answered readily. "What about *Drink to Me Only With Thine Eyes*? You always performed it very well, as I recall."

"I will if I can remember the words." During the past four years, she had never once sung the old love song, for it had reminded her too much of him. "I know it was a particular favorite of yours."

Brandon still clasped her hand. Now he raised it to his lips and gazed over it with a look she might have mistaken for sweet yearning, if she did not know better.

"Only when *you* sang it," he replied in a melting murmur.

Cassandra knew she should discourage him from making such remarks and gestures. They could too easily be misinterpreted as romantic.

They made it harder for her to remember that he could never be hers.

If he heard Cassandra sing that song, Brandon believed it would tell him whether she still cared for him and if he had a second chance to make her his.

Mr. Martin's advice had given him hope. Cassandra's behavior this evening had strengthened that hope. Yet he could not deny a faint edge of wistfulness to her merriment. Was it only the anticipation of their parting? Or could it be a warning that his heart ought to heed if it did not want old wounds torn open again?

As the party filed into the Martins' parlor, where Imogene and Edward were enthroned on the two best armchairs, Brandon tried to dismiss his doubts by recalling the meal they'd just eaten. Over the years he had dined on pheasant and swan prepared by the most accomplished chefs. None could rival the flavor of Mrs. Martin's goose, seasoned with the rare spice of Cassandra's company. Now he looked forward to dancing with her more than he had anticipated anything in a great while.

Brandon swiftly scanned the parlor. The only remaining seats were under the window beside Mrs. Davis. Two nights ago, he and Cassandra had perched there side-by-side with the greatest reluctance. His present attitude was quite the opposite. He wondered if, once again, Mrs. Martin might have had a hand in nudging them together. If so, he owed her a debt he could never hope to repay.

An enchanting effusion of color blossomed in Cassandra's cheeks, when she noted the seating arrangements. Did the starry shimmer in her dark eyes mean she welcomed the opportunity to nestle beside him?

"Who will take the first turn at entertaining us?" asked Imogene with a regal air. Clearly she was enjoying her role as Queen of Twelfth Night.

To Brandon's surprise, the taciturn stagecoach guard volunteered to sing for them. In honor of his two brothers who served in the Royal Navy, he performed the sailors' anthem, *Heart of Oak*, in a fine rumbling bass. He invited any of the others who knew the words to join him on the chorus.

After a round of enthusiastic applause, Mrs. Davis followed

with a spirited recitation of *The Castaway*.

As the poem rose toward its dramatic conclusion, Cassandra cupped her hand around Brandon's ear and whispered, "What will *you* perform?"

Her question flustered him almost as much as the delicious tickle of her breath upon his ear. He had been so concentrated on the prospect of her singing that he'd spared no thought for what he might contribute to the program. He gave a mute shrug and began to think on the matter.

He would not be so cruel as to subject them to his singing. Any stories he knew were not particularly suitable for mixed company. He considered trying to beg off but he doubted Queen Imogene would permit such a lapse. That left only a recitation.

While the company applauded Mrs. Davis, and Perkins followed with an eerie ghost story which he swore was true, Brandon reviewed the modest number of poems he knew by heart. Might there be one capable of conveying his feelings to Cassandra, as he hoped her song would do to him?

Mr. Martin went next, tuning up his fiddle to serenade them with the familiar *Country Gardens*. He soon had everyone humming along.

"Who will go next?" asked Imogene after the applause had died away. "Brandon, what about you?"

"I beg a little more time, Your Majesty. I am still trying to decide what to perform."

His cousin nodded then moved on. "What about you Lady Cassandra? Or are you undecided as well?"

"I am quite decided." Cassandra rose and moved to the spot in front of the hearth where the others had stood. "Only reluctant to follow on the heels of superior performers."

"Tosh!" The word popped out before Brandon could contain it. "The lady is too modest. I have heard her sing and I can assure you it will be a treat."

Imogene looked less pleased than she had until then. "Do not keep us in suspense then, Lady Cassandra. Favor us with your selection."

"Drink to me only with thine eyes and I will pledge with mine." She began rather uncertainly, but when her gaze met Brandon's, her tone grew more assured. *"Or leave a kiss within the cup and I'll not ask for wine."*

Listening to the old love song, it seemed to Brandon as if all the other guests melted away, leaving only Cassandra and him. Every sweet word from her lips pealed with perfect sincerity and he knew they were meant for him alone. When the final note died away, he led the loudest and longest applause yet that evening.

Cassandra made a self-conscious curtsey then returned to her place at Brandon's sides — the place where she would always belong.

One by one, the rest of the company were urged to take their turn while Brandon racked his brains for a suitable response to Cassandra's musical declaration. Only when Imogene insisted he must do something so they could move on to the dancing did inspiration strike.

Flashing Cassandra a grin, he bounded up and launched into his favorite sonnet. *"My mistress' eyes are nothing like the sun."* His dry, off-hand delivery of the lines mocked extravagant protestations of admiration. *"Coral is far more red than her lips ..."*

From the moment he'd first read the poem at school, he had admired Shakespeare for daring to tell the truth about lovers' flattery. When his friends had fallen in love and praised their sweethearts to the skies, he had skewered them with this sly sonnet. Then he'd fallen in love with Cassandra Whitney and all his cynicism flew out the window, to be replaced by lavish poetry. He had placed her on such a dangerously high pedestal, that she could not help but fall.

Tonight he appreciated the sonnet in a whole new way. The lady it described was no immaculate paragon who would never soil her hands with household chores, feel secretly ashamed of her father, or speak a single false word. She was a human being with flaws and insecurities but no less dear for all that.

A few brief days in these humble surroundings had made Brandon recognize and appreciate Cassandra for the woman she was — not a flawless goddess but a fine, generous person trying to do the right thing in a difficult situation. He strove to infuse every wise, forgiving word of Shakespeare's sonnet with that realization. He hoped Cassandra would understand.

"And yet, by heaven," he concluded with a fond flourish, *"I think my love more fair than any she belied with false compare."*

Brandon was vaguely aware of his audience chuckling over his recitation, but the only response that mattered was Cassandra's. She smiled and laughed in all the proper places then clapped heartily when he finished. Yet he glimpsed a faint suggestion of regret beneath her amusement. It made him wonder if she had taken a different meaning than the one he intended.

If so, he must make certain she understood.

"That was fine bit of entertainment, if I do say so," Mr. Martin declared. "I doubt you would find better between London and Bath. Now if our king and queen would care to lead off the first dance."

He tucked the fiddle under his chin and struck up a lively tune. "Let us begin with *The Indian Queen*. Though for this evening perhaps we should rename it *The Twelfth Night Queen*."

Imogene bounced up from her chair and extended a hand to Edward. "Shall we then? It is our duty as king and queen."

The lad grinned and blushed but accepted her invitation readily enough.

Meanwhile Brandon strode toward the window seat before any of the other men could reach it.

"You promised me a dance," he reminded Cassandra. "I mean to claim it before you are overwhelmed with requests."

"Of course I remember." She rose and joined him as second couple to his cousin and the footman. "Though I do not believe my company will be as sought after as you expect."

The older folk seemed content to let the younger ones have the floor for the first dance.

Mr. Martin had made an excellent choice, Brandon reflected as they began to dance. The steps were simple enough and did not require a great deal of space to execute. His only regret was that the dance did not require him to perform any two-handed turns with Cassandra.

No sooner had the first dance concluded than the stage-coach driver asked Cassandra to be his partner for the next. Reluctantly, Brandon surrendered her and withdrew to the far corner of the parlor where Mrs. Martin sat.

He approached her with a gallant bow. "Will you do me the honor of the next dance, ma'am?"

"With pleasure, Sir Brandon, though I shall not be able to match the grace of your first partner. You and she make a handsome couple, I must say. I hope to see the two of you dance together often tonight."

Brandon could not help smiling. "I shall endeavor to gratify your wish, ma'am."

He was as good as his word, dancing several more times with Cassandra, though far less often than he would have liked. If it would not have violated all propriety, he'd have bribed every other man present a hundred pounds to claim *their* turns with the lady.

As the evening wore on, he found himself standing beside Mrs. Martin again. He was about to ask her to take another turn with him when she nodded toward the dancers.

"Lady Cassandra looks rather flushed, don't you think?" Their hostess sounded concerned, though Brandon approved the rosy glow of Cassandra's complexion. "Someone ought to take her out to the kitchen where it is cooler and see that she gets a drink. Could I prevail upon you, Sir Brandon?"

"I should be happy to help ma'am." If he had not feared her husband would take it amiss, he might have kissed Mrs. Martin then and there. "After all, we would not want Lady Cassandra to get overheated and fall ill."

Their hostess beamed up at him. "I knew I could depend upon you."

Brandon edged around the perimeter of the room until he reached the passageway to the kitchen. He waited for the dance to finish, then beckoned Cassandra to join him. "Mrs. Martin thinks you look flushed. I am under strict orders to escort you to the kitchen to cool off."

"Are you, indeed?" Cassandra pressed her hands to her cheeks. "I could do with a drink. I have not danced so much in …"

"Four years?" Brandon suggested as he led her toward the kitchen. "Oddly enough, that is how long it has been since I last enjoyed myself so much."

"It is?" She sounded doubtful.

He gave a decisive nod. "I would not exaggerate. You know what store I set by the truth."

The kitchen was cooler than the parlor — dimmer and quieter too.

Brandon turned to face Cassandra. "I enjoyed your song very much. I fancied you were addressing its words to me. Indeed, I wished you were."

This broad hint regarding his feelings did not seem to please her as he'd hoped. Her gaze fell and she caught her full lower lip between her teeth. "I wish that were possible, but—"

Before she could say anything more, Brandon pressed his forefinger to her lips. "Let there be no *buts* tonight. This is Twelfth Night, when three kings followed a star halfway around the world to bring priceless gifts to an infant born in a stable. On such a night, surely anything we want enough must be possible."

Strong-willed though he knew Cassandra to be, she did not resist him. Instead she submitted as if she were powerless against his gentle touch. For his part, Brandon had no power to resist the urge that took possession of him. Lifting his finger, he leaned toward her and replaced it with his lips.

This was the kiss he'd been saving for their betrothal — the kiss he had been deprived of four years ago. The desire for it had lingered on his lips ever since, subtly poisoning every bite or sip he took in and every word he let out. Tonight, win or lose, he must have it!

Her lips yielded to the tender pressure of his. They fell open just enough to release a soft gasp of surprise ... and ... joy? Then to his delight, she raised one hand to caress his cheek and began to kiss him back with innocent ardor that made his breath catch and his heart skip.

Time slowed like thick, golden resin on a cold day. Brandon would gladly have been caught forever in the moment as it turned to amber.

Then a sharp gasp pierced their sweet bubble of isolation. Cassandra stiffened and pulled away from him. She turned toward the sound, just as his did.

Brandon's gaze collided with his cousin's shocked, accusing stare.

"What is the meaning of this?" she demanded as if she truly was his sovereign and he owed her an explanation.

But he did not, Brandon reminded himself. He was doing nothing wrong. Indeed he had never done anything that felt so right.

"I think the meaning should be perfectly obvious, Imogene. I am in love with Lady Cassandra and intend to propose to her again, if you will give us a moment's privacy."

Mrs. Martin appeared at his cousin's elbow just then and tried to make her leave them in peace. But Imogene wrenched her arm from the woman's touch. "What about Miss Reynolds?" she demanded.

His cousin's question made Brandon's insides contract into a cold little ball of lead that plummeted into his toes.

But that was nothing to the dismay that gripped him when Cassandra echoed his cousin's words, more in sorrow than anger. "Tell us, Sir Brandon. What about Miss Reynolds?"

Chapter Fifteen

A TEMPEST OF conflicting emotions raged within Cassandra's heart as she stood in the Martins' kitchen with Brandon's kiss still tingling upon her lips.

Part of her longed to seek comfort in the shelter of his protective, tender embrace. Yet her rigorous conscience warned her she would find no sanctuary there, only confusion and perhaps more shame.

The contempt with which Imogene Calvert regarded her stung Cassandra's pride like caustic lye. What made it all the worse was that she could not deny her wrongdoing. She had allowed Brandon to kiss her. Then she had kissed him back with ardent abandon even though she knew he intended to marry Miss Reynolds. Deluding herself that Brandon wanted nothing more than friendship, she had led him on all evening to do something they would both regret.

Did he love her, as he claimed to his cousin, and truly wish to marry her? Or was he only trying to protect her from the consequences of her folly by offering to do the honorable thing? Knowing his chivalrous nature, she feared it must be the latter. But how could she subject him to such a union when a much more suitable match awaited him elsewhere?

Were the same thoughts racing through Brandon's mind as his mouth opened and closed but emitted no sound?

At last he mastered his voice to address his cousin. "None of this is any of your concern, Imogene, particularly my intentions toward Isabella Reynolds! That is a matter I wish to discuss with Lady Cassandra, if you will give us a little privacy by returning to the parlor."

"I will not!" Miss Calvert's grey eyes flashed with glints of steel. "Not while you are under the spell of this nefarious creature! Only this morning she swore that she had no designs upon you. Yet she has been throwing herself at your head ever since. You always go on about how important it is to tell the truth. How can you think of marrying such a conniving liar?"

Cassandra flinched from Miss Calvert's harsh accusation which she feared was far too true, in spite of her efforts to persuade herself otherwise.

Brandon took a step toward his cousin, stabbing the air with the forefinger he had recently rested against Cassandra's lips. "You will take back that vile insult at once if you wish us to remain friends, Imogene. The lady is not a liar! She did not have designs upon me nor did she pursue me — quite the opposite, in fact. That does not mean she has no feelings for me or could not learn to care for me."

Learn to care? If she had needed teaching, Brandon's gallant defense of her would have provided a compelling lesson. If only she was worthy of his staunch support.

But did he truly believe what he had told his cousin? Poisonous doubt whispered in the back of Cassandra's mind. Or was he only trying to prevent any cruel gossip that might arise if she agreed to marry him — gossip that would reflect ill upon him and their family?

Well he need not fret about such things. She had no intention of saddling him with a wife whose only dowry would be debt and dishonor. She had protected him before from her father's selfish rapacity. Now she must protect him from his own misplaced charity.

"Please, Brandon." She placed a restraining hand on his arm, in part because she could not resist the urge to touch him for perhaps the last time. "Do not quarrel with your cousin on my account. You do not need to defend me."

He turned toward her but before he could reply, Imogene Calvert unleashed her final blast. "Why will you not see her for what she is, cuz? Ask her why she is going to visit her aunt, why don't you? There is some secret behind it that she does not want you to know. The other morning, when she thought I was sleeping, I heard her tell her friend not to mention the reason. No doubt it is some scandal she means to conceal until she is certain she had secured you. Promise me you will not propose to her until you have learned the truth!"

Cassandra shrank from the look in his eyes — wounded, disillusioned sorrow that cut her to the core. He believed his cousin's accusation, as well he should. What scandal did he imagine she had committed to merit her exile to rural Somerset and the strict, respectable guardianship of her great-aunt?

Of course her secret was nothing so sordid, but how could she tell him that? Learning of her straitened circumstances might make Brandon more determined than ever to stand by her, even when it was clear he could never fully trust her.

Mrs. Martin's simmering exasperation with Imogene Calvert finally reached a boil. "I reckon you have said more than enough, young lady. Now come away at once and let these two sort out matters for themselves."

Miss Calvert crossed her arms in front of her and fired off a defiant reply. "I told you, I have no intention of leaving my cousin alone with that creature. She will only get around him with more of her simpering lies!"

For the first time since Brandon's cousin had begun to berate her, Cassandra took offense. She might not have been as open and truthful with him as she should, but she had never *simpered*!

Clearly Mrs. Martin was not about to let her young nemesis have the last word. "I will thank you to remember that you are a guest in *my* house, Miss Calvert. If you refuse to do as I ask then you are welcome to sleep in the barn tonight!"

"The barn?" Imogene squealed. "You wouldn't!"

The farmer's wife leveled a stony stare at her. "Just you try me."

"It's not fair!" Imogene stormed, though it was clear she was not prepared to risk Mrs. Martin's threat. "I am only trying to save my cousin from a dreadful mistake."

She began inching out of the kitchen. "Please, Brandon, do not let her persuade you to do something you are sure to regret for the rest of your life!"

If only Brandon's cousin knew how unnecessary her warning was, Cassandra reflected. *She* had no intention of persuading the baronet to do anything he might regret. The harder task would be to keep him from persuading her to heed the pleadings of her wayward heart rather than the righteous dictates of her conscience.

"I thought she would never leave." Brandon muttered as fiddle music from the parlor drowned out his cousin's voice.

Though he tried to sound and feel relieved at Imogene's going, part of him was not. Now there was nothing to keep him from speaking to Cassandra when caution urged him to fly as far away from her as he could get.

The sweet taste of her kiss still lingered on his lips and his heart throbbed with his reawakened love for her. Only a moment ago, he had declared that love and his intention to propose to her again. But how could he? He and Cassandra had both concealed important information from one another and they both knew it.

Could there be any surer sign that they might be doomed to repeat the disastrous mistakes of his parents? Were all marriages like that in the end — a sham of happiness hiding deceit and misery? Certainly Cassandra's experiences bore out that cynical notion. Brandon did not want such a union for them and especially not for any innocent children they might bring into such a benighted family.

But how could he turn his back on Cassandra after he had compromised her reputation with that kiss and declared his intention to ask for her hand? Must he choose between a lifetime of regret and a lifetime of dishonor?

"Come …" He motioned her toward the table, still laid with the remains of their Twelfth Night feast. That jolly meal now seemed so long ago. "We need to talk, you and I."

"Do we?" Cassandra marched toward the table but instead of taking a seat she began to clear the dishes away with unfeeling diligence. "Why? It is clear what took place this evening and it is scarcely a wonder, given the circumstances. Would it not be best for everyone simply to pretend it never happened?"

A dozen questions clamored in Brandon's thoughts in response to hers. He hardly knew where to begin. "What do *you* suppose took place here this evening? Why is it not to be wondered at and what circumstances are you referring to? Why would it be best to pretend nothing happened? You know my attitude toward pretense when it comes to matters of affection."

"Indeed I do." Cassandra gave a mirthless little chuckle that seemed to belittle his deepest principles. Could she possibly be the same woman who had melted in his arms such a short time ago? "It is the same as your rigid, impractical attitude toward the occasional innocent falsehood."

She seemed to sneer at him and his beliefs. Where was the woman he thought he had grown to know so well during these past few days? Had Cassandra pretended to be someone she clearly was not, or had he deceived himself about her?

"The kiss that took place between us was a foolish mistake for which no one is to blame," Cassandra continued as she went about the task of tidying the kitchen. "It was simply the result of being cooped up together again after all these years. Who could blame us for fancying old feelings had revived under such circumstances?"

"It was not a fancy!" Brandon grasped her hands and drew her away from the table, to make her give more than a crumb of attention to the vital matter they were discussing. "I meant what I told Imogene. I love you, Cassandra and I want to marry you. You made me believe you could return my feelings. I know you once cared for me enough to refuse my proposal in a misguided effort to protect me. Is that what you are trying to do now?"

She refused to meet his gaze but pulled herself up tall and proud. Then she shrugged her arms from his grasp the way she might have brushed a bit of dirt from her sleeve. "I cannot deny I was quite smitten with you at one time. But that was four years ago. A great deal has changed since then."

"Not my feelings for you!" Brandon insisted, though he could not keep an edge of doubt from sharpening his tone. Had he continued to love her all these years and did he love the woman she had become? Or was he still infatuated with his ideal of her — the perfect lady-love whose eyes were like the sun and lips like coral? The goddess whose feet scarcely touched the ground and whose lips never spoke a false word?

"I am certain you believe that or you would not say it," Cassandra replied. Was she patronizing him now? "But the fact remains that you planned to propose to Miss Reynolds. If not for an unfortunate accident of the weather, you might be engaged to the lady by now."

Brandon longed to deny her claim, but how could he? Instead he took a different tack. "Imogene told you that, I suppose. She had no right to! I assure you I told her no such thing."

Cassandra was not so easily put off. "But it is true, is it not?"

"I was considering the possibility," he began, only to meet her doubtful look. "Oh very well, I did intend to propose to Miss Reynolds, but only because I had given up any hope of you. And because I need to produce an heir."

Her fine, dark brows rose. "Is that not the case for every gentleman of property?"

"I suppose so. But for me it is particularly vital." He shrank from confessing the reason when she was keeping a secret from him. Had she raised the subject of Isabella Reynolds, hoping it would distract him from the mystery surrounding her visit to Noughtly Hall?

He must tell her, he decided at last. Perhaps then she would understand how important it was that they be able to confide in one another. "You may recall what I told you about my parents' marriage. In recent years, I learned that they were both unfaithful. My mother flaunted her affairs under my father's nose, yet for the longest time, he never suspected the depth of her disloyalty."

Cassandra's eyes widened. His revelation seemed to shake her frosty composure. "Do you mean to say your brother is not …?"

"Not a true Calvert." Brandon gave a bitter nod. "I always wondered why our mother favored him so much, while I could do nothing right in her eyes. Before my father died he made me promise to start a family so my brother would not inherit a title and estate to which he has no right."

"I see." Cassandra murmured. "You were in such haste to obey your father's instructions that you could not wait for Miss Reynolds but felt you must propose to the first likely lady who crossed your path. Excuse me if I choose not to be flattered."

"It was not like that!" Brandon plowed his fingers through his hair. "Why must you twist everything to put me in the wrong? You remind me of—"

He stopped himself but not soon enough.

"Your mother?" Cassandra whispered.

For a moment her mask slipped and he glimpsed behind the unruffled facade to much more intense, complex emotions she sought to conceal. If only he could interpret them.

He gave a curt nod to which Cassandra responded by shaking her head. "I do not mean to put you in the wrong. What happened is not your fault. Nor do I blame you for wanting to keep your intentions toward Miss Reynolds private, especially if you were not certain you would propose to her. But do you not see? This promise you made to your father was on your mind when we were unexpectedly thrown together. It is perfectly reasonable that you should believe your former feelings toward me had been revived. I almost believed it myself and I did not have such a compelling reason as you."

"What makes you so certain they were not?"

A wistful smile played across her lips, disappearing as quickly as it came. "It is tempting to believe that, but unlikely, don't you think?"

Before Brandon could disagree she pressed on. "Even if we still cared for one another after all these years or fell back in love in a matter of days, what chance would we have for a successful marriage? Coming from the families we do — it would take a miracle."

He wanted to contradict her but reason would not let him. Whether the qualities required for a happy marriage were passed down through the blood or whether the necessary skills were learned from observation, he and Cassandra were both at a grave disadvantage. He would be a fool to deny it.

"What about your reputation?" Brandon felt on much firmer ground with that aspect of the situation. "Only the vilest blackguard would threaten a lady's reputation with a kiss like that then refuse to marry her. We must wed. It is a matter of honor."

Immediately he sensed his words were having the opposite effect than the one for which he'd hoped.

Any trace of softness or suppressed longing disappeared from Cassandra's countenance, driven away by proud severity. "You need not fret about your honor, Sir Brandon. I thought that must be the true motive for your insistence we wed. You have not refused to rescue my reputation. I have refused to be rescued. I would rather risk celibate disgrace than marital misery. Besides, I doubt either Mrs. Martin or your cousin will breathe a word of what they saw. Consequently, my reputation and your honor are not in such grave danger as you imagine."

Reason warned him to accept her answer and be grateful to her for releasing him from his obligation. But he could not prevent himself from offering up one last feeble inducement. "I would do anything in my power to ensure you were not miserable in our marriage. I would do anything to make you happy."

Cassandra remained unswayed, which she demonstrated by promptly turning away from him. "I know you would, and I would try to do the same. But I do not believe it is in anyone's power to make another happy. My misery would come from knowing I had kept you from a more suitable marriage by taking advantage of your honor and obligation to your family."

Why must she harp on those? They were only his *excuses* for wanting to marry her, not his reasons. He would have asked her, but something else she'd said kept him silent. Deep down, he knew she was right that no one could make another happy, just as no one could compel the love of another. He had tried all his life to make his mother love him, to no avail. That failure had bred heartache. The last thing he wanted was to repeat that destructive pattern with Cassandra.

After a pause she spoke again in a softer tone. "You deserve a wife you can respect and trust."

"I do respect you!" Brandon wanted to insist he trusted her, too. He had tried. If only she had not made it so difficult.

"For the moment, perhaps." She fired the words back over her shoulder. "But respect cannot survive in the absence of trust. You have shown admirable restraint not to inquire about my reasons for visiting Aunt Augusta in Bath. Yet I know you must want an explanation."

"I want you to tell me of your own accord because you trust that you *can* tell me the truth and it will make no difference to my feelings for you. I swear it will not, whatever is the matter."

She shook her head. "I can only tell you that it is not as dreadful as you suspect. But I am certain it would alter your feelings toward me."

"I cannot imagine how that is possible if the circumstances are as innocent as you claim. Why can you not tell me and allow me to decide for myself, the way you ought to have done four years ago?"

Why was he arguing and pleading when he had so

many doubts himself? A wise man would seize this opportunity to extricate himself from a situation that threatened more heartache.

"I *wish* I could tell you." Cassandra's voice fell to a pensive murmur. Her shoulders slumped in defeat. "But it is not in my power. It is not in my nature."

He marched around in front of her to make her face him. "You are quite determined to refuse my proposal for the second time after you admit regretting that you refused me before?"

"You never made me a formal proposal this evening." Her glance flitted this way and that, refusing to meet his. "You only declared your intention to do it."

"Do not quibble!" The words burst out of Brandon, louder and fiercer than he's intended.

Cassandra gave a violent start and shrank from him in a way that tore at Brandon's heart. But she soon gathered her composure and struck back. "Very well, then. Since you are so fond of the truth, here it is. I *did* regret refusing you four years ago and I expect I shall regret refusing you now. But I believe any regret I suffer as a consequence will be less than if I accept your offer."

How could he argue with that? If so much tension and hostility bristled between them during the mere *discussion* of marriage, how could they hope to be happy together? "Then there is nothing left to be said."

His despairing resignation seemed to soothe the antagonism his opposition had inflamed. When Cassandra answered, her tone was once again soft and wistful. "Only one thing. I am sorry with all my heart that I could not give you a different answer. I wish you all the happiness in the world with Miss Reynolds. I hope she will prove worthy of you in every way."

The fond luster in her dark eyes and the sorrowful affection in her tone made him care for her in ways she refused to accept.

It was too frustrating and heartbreaking for Brandon to

bear. He must get away from this place at once. He must get his life back on the clear, straight path it had been heading before the storm and his encounter with Lady Cassandra Whitney threw it off course.

"This is goodbye then." He turned and strode away, ignoring the pleas of his heart.

To himself, he muttered. "I pray it will be our last."

Chapter Sixteen

"WHAT ARE YOU moping about now, Cassandra?" Great-aunt Augusta's sharp query crashed in upon her private thoughts like a bludgeon blow to a wounded limb. "I must say, when I invited you here to act as my companion, it was in the belief that your youthful company would prove stimulating. Instead it has been quite the reverse. I have had more animated conversation at funerals."

The two women sat in the smallest sitting room of Noughtly Hall with a good fire going, yet the chill of this cold, snowy winter seemed to penetrate the very marrow of Cassandra's bones. She had only been here for a fortnight, yet already it felt like several long months. Only the arrival of letters from her sisters lifted her gloom. But the continuing heavy snow had disrupted the flow of mail more than once.

She considered using the dull weather and enforced seclusion as an excuse for her low spirits, but her ever-present thoughts of Sir Brandon Calvert prevented her. Her reluctance to be a burden to him had made it impossible for them to be together. But at least she could honor her feelings for him by trying to be as truthful as he would wish.

She arranged her features into the best imitation of a smile that she could manage. "I am sorry to have disappointed you, Aunt Augusta. I shall endeavor to do better. Would you like me to read to you? Or perhaps we could move to the music room so I could play the pianoforte."

She could scarcely afford to jeopardize her position here. It was her only means of providing Evie with an opportunity to seek the kind of love that had eluded her sisters.

Had love truly eluded her? An inner voice of truth challenged Cassandra. The voice sounded like Brandon's. Had love eluded her, or had she run away from it because it threatened her precious pride and self-reliance?

"I am tired of being read to," the viscountess complained, "particularly in that lifeless monotone. Neither do I wish to quit this room since it is the warmest in the house. Would a little conversation be too much to ask? Tell me more about the time you spent snowbound at that farmhouse. It has the makings of a rather diverting tale."

For the first time since coming to Noughtly Hall, Cassandra truly looked at her great-aunt. Not for her the light muslin dresses and natural hair styles currently in fashion. She continued to wear a towering, powdered wig and the elaborately hooped, corseted gown of a more formal era. Cassandra could not imagine Lady Augusta ever crossing the threshold of a farm cottage.

She knew her great-aunt had made an arranged marriage to a wealthy nobleman many years her senior. Their only child had died at a young age and her husband not long after … of a broken heart, perhaps? In nearly fifty years since then, the viscountess had lived in comfortable splendor … and bitter loneliness?

"I will tell you," Cassandra replied, "if you will first tell me why you never remarried."

The instant the words were out, she wondered how she had dared to ask such an impertinent question. She expected to be roundly rebuked for it.

Much to her surprise, her great-aunt answered as she might have to a confidante. "It was not for lack of suitors, of that you may be certain." She nodded toward a portrait of herself above the mantel. "I was accounted rather handsome in my youth and not without accomplishment."

Her stern countenance softened as she recalled those lost years.

Cassandra's lips curved in their first true smile since she had left the Martins' farm. "You must have been a most eligible prospect indeed. Did you break many hearts when you refused all the proposals you received?"

"Hardly!" The viscountess gave an unladylike snort of laughter. "I disappointed a considerable number of ambitions, no doubt, since my fortune, estates and connections were the true objects of my suitors' desire. That, of course, was why I rejected their proposals."

That made sense, Cassandra reflected. Why should a woman of independence and property want to surrender both to a husband she could never be certain cared anything for her?

"There was one, though …" the viscountess mused, perhaps not aware that she had spoken aloud.

"Tell me about him," Cassandra leaned forward in her chair. Who would have thought she and her great-aunt might share a common bond of romantic regrets?

"I would have accepted him if he had so much as hinted at a proposal." Her ladyship's eyes took on a misty, distant look that made the years melt away from her features. "But he was too proud to take a wife of greater consequence than he. In the end, he went away to India to make his fortune. I always believed it was so he could return and marry me without any suspicion of fortune-hunting."

Cassandra sympathized with that proud young man. If only it were possible for a woman to *earn* her fortune in a respectable way, she would have been tempted to follow his example. "He sounds like a fine man. Whatever became of him?"

The viscountess rose abruptly and strode to the window to stare out at the barren, white garden. "He worked himself to death in that dreadful climate."

"Poor man!" Cassandra cried.

"Proud young fool, you mean," the viscountess rapped out in her accustomed brusque tone. Yet the hoarseness of her voice betrayed affection and regret. "If he cared for me so much, why did he throw away the happy years we might have had … the family?"

"What else could he do?" Cassandra could not resist the urge to defend the young gentleman who had died long before she was born. "You would not have wanted him to be like all the others you despised. If he had married you with no fortune of his own, you might have come to despise him in the end."

"Never!" Great-aunt Augusta turned back from the window, her face pale as a ghost but her eyes blazing. "If he cared for me, he should have known I would place a higher value on his company than on any plot of land or pile of gold."

For a moment, Cassandra glimpsed the lingering grief the formidable old lady had hidden so long under her irascible facade. The prospect of Brandon carrying such a burden of unhappiness grieved her.

"Forgive me Auntie." Cassandra rose and backed toward the door. She did not wish to give way to her feelings in front of the viscountess. "Perhaps the gentleman was only trying to spare you … to protect you."

Before the viscountess could announce her intention to send her impudent great-niece packing back to Rosemeade, Cassandra fled the sitting room.

Fortunately her composure had not entirely deserted her when she met Mrs. Davis carrying a letter. "The post has arrived, Lady Cassandra."

In spite of everything, her spirits rose a little. Perhaps if she made a particular effort to divert Great-aunt Augusta, the viscountess would allow Viola or Miranda to come for a visit.

"Thank you for bringing it." Cassandra took the letter and glanced at the unfamiliar handwriting. Who besides her sisters or Letty knew she was visiting Noughtly Hall?

The thought made her too curious to retreat all the way to her bedchamber to read it. Instead she broke the wax seal immediately and scanned the mysterious missive.

"Oh my!" she cried aloud when she realized who had

written it.

"Is anything the matter?" Mrs. Davis asked in an anxious tone.

Cassandra shook her head. "I am surprised, that's all. This letter is from Miss Calvert at Everleigh."

"Indeed." Mrs. Davis's eyebrows flew up. "I did not think the two of you had parted on such friendly terms as to correspond."

"Nor did I." Cassandra recalled the Calverts' abrupt departure from the Martins' cottage on Twelfth Night.

They had only gone as far as the inn at Cherhill to spend the rest of the night. It had been a wrench to part from Brandon again under even worse circumstances than they had met. But there had been an element of relief as well. After what had transpired in the Martins' kitchen, Cassandra was certain Imogene Calvert would have refused to share a bed with her and Mrs. Davis that night.

"Distance appears to have softened her hostility toward me. She apologizes for not being more civil."

"As well she should," Mrs. Davis muttered. A badly-concealed glint in her eyes betrayed her curiosity about the contents of the letter.

It was impossible to tell how much she'd guessed about Cassandra and Brandon's history and what had recently transpired between them, for she was the soul of discretion. Yet something in the housekeeper's manner suggested that she knew more than she would ever reveal.

Cassandra glanced back at Miss Calvert's letter.

"*Ever since Twelfth Night,*" the young lady wrote, "*I have been burdened with regret over how I misjudged your character. When Brandon told me you rejected his proposal that night, it made me realize your motives were pure. The more I thought about it, the more I began to wonder if you'd had a good reason for refusing him the first time.*"

Cassandra's eyes widened. That insight showed greater perception than she expected from Imogene Calvert.

"*I hope you can forgive my rudeness and ingratitude,*" the letter continued, "*though I understand if my conduct has made that impossible.*"

What a change a fortnight had wrought in Brandon's cousin! Then again, that was five times longer than they'd been snowbound at the Martins' farm. In that brief span of time, Miss Calvert had gone from fawning over Cassandra to detesting her.

A dismaying thought made Cassandra's breath catch. Did Imogene Calvert suddenly feel more charitable toward her because Brandon was now safely engaged to Miss Reynolds?

"Is it bad news?" asked Mrs. Davis. "You look pale just now."

"Not at all." Cassandra tried to make light of her distress. "Perhaps I am turning blue from the cold."

It was not exactly a lie, she assured herself. She had not yet read the news she feared. Even if it were true, such information should be cause for rejoicing, not dejection. She *would* rejoice for Brandon's happiness once she grew accustomed to the idea.

"Perhaps you should go check on her ladyship," Cassandra suggested, fearing she might not be able to conceal her dismay from Mrs. Davis when she read the fateful announcement. "Tell her I will return to keep her company shortly."

"Of course, my lady." The housekeeper bobbed a hasty curtsey then headed off.

Cassandra drew a deep breath and lifted a silent prayer for courage to face the news and behave correctly. Then she forced herself to read on.

A moment later she flew into the sitting room, her heart racing and her breath coming in shallow little gasps. The viscountess and the housekeeper turned to stare at her.

Before either of them could demand the reason for her abrupt entrance, Cassandra held out the letter with a trembling hand. "I was wrong Mrs. Davis. It *is* bad news. The very worst! Auntie may I have a carriage to go at once to Everleigh?

Miss Calvert writes that her cousin is very ill. She fears he may not live!"

"You don't look well at all, cuz." Imogene hovered around Brandon as he tried to read his newspaper. Not that there was much news to report except how all the snowstorms had brought much of the country to a halt. "Don't you think you ought to go lie down?"

"Why?" He lowered his copy of the *Bath Chronicle* enough to peer over it at his cousin with narrowed eyes. "Do you want me out of the way so you can throw yourself at young Sandiford without hindrance?"

"I do not!" Imogene looked highly offended — a sure sign, in Brandon's experience, that she was up to something. "I have given up any notion of Lord Sandiford. He is a dry stick for such a young man and so disapproving of anything the least bit amusing. I am certain he would make me quite miserable."

Brandon dropped his newspaper to his lap. "It took you long enough to come to that conclusion, but I believe you are right. I am sorry this house party has not lived up to your expectations."

Imogene dismissed his sympathy with a toss of her golden curls. "Don't fret for me. Mr. Geoffreys is very nice and Lord Holbrook. I feel much worse for you. I can see now that Miss Reynolds is not at all the right woman for you. I wish I had not spoiled things between you and Lady Cassandra."

"You did not spoil anything." A sigh escaped Brandon in spite of his best effort to contain it. "You were the least of our problems."

Ever since they'd driven away from the Martins' farm, he had been plagued by questions, doubts and regrets. Cassandra had given every indication of caring for him yet she had refused to do the one thing that would insure his happiness. And what was the great mystery of her visit to Noughtly? Was she trying to protect him again, as she had from her father's pernicious influence? Did she not understand he could bear any other calamity better than that of losing her? After many sleepless nights, he had finally come to a decision.

"If it makes you feel any better, Imogene, I have resolved to call in at Noughtly on our way home to see if the passage of a little time might have eased some of Lady Cassandra's objections."

"What a fine idea." His cousin looked more alarmed than pleased with his plan.

If he lived to be a hundred, would he ever understand women? He would give anything if Cassandra would permit him the opportunity to understand her.

"I still say you ought to take a nap," Imogene continued with a hint of desperation. "You look dreadfully tired. You would not want to delay our departure by falling ill."

"Will it satisfy you if I recline on the chaise lounge to read my paper?" Brandon knew the futility of trying to put his cousin off once she got an idea in her head.

"Yes, I believe that will do." She took his elbow and helped him from the chair as if he were quite ancient.

Brandon settled on the chaise lounge and returned to his reading. But the news was so very dull and his sleepless nights were finally catching up with him.

The drone of conversation from other members of the house party playing cards in the adjoining room lulled him into a doze. He was vaguely aware of someone easing the newspaper from his hands then covering his lower limbs with a blanket. With a decision made regarding Cassandra, Brandon surrendered to his fatigue.

Some time later he was violently jolted awake by a woman's cries and a soft, cool hand upon his forehead.

"I came the moment I read your letter!" The lady sounded quite distraught. What letter was she referring to? "I hope I am not too late. What is he doing down here? He should be in bed, attended by a physician. He does not feel feverish. Has he been bled?"

Cassandra? Brandon struggled to open his eyes. If he was

dreaming about her, he did not want to wake up. But he could not bear to hear her so upset.

"Brandon, dearest, can you hear me?" Her hand ran over his forehead and through his hair in an anxious caress. "Please, my love, you must not give up! I cannot bear to lose you forever. I was a proud, stubborn fool. I should have told you the truth. How could I have thrown away a precious second chance with you? If that is what made you ill, my darling, I do not know how I shall ever forgive myself!"

It must be a dream, though quite the most vivid one he had ever experienced. Brandon had almost convinced himself of the fact, when he became aware of other voices in the background.

"Who *is* that madwoman and what is she doing in my house?"

"She looks like one of the Whitney sisters."

"Is Sir Brandon ill? He looked well enough at breakfast."

Then he heard Imogene. "Out, all of you, out! Leave them in peace. I will explain everything."

The sitting room door shut quite forcibly.

Suddenly he knew he was not dreaming. But he had an idea what was going on. Did he dare tell Cassandra she was the victim of a deception? Tempting as it was to play the invalid and take advantage of her concern, Brandon could not bear to prolong her anxiety.

He opened his eyes and seized her hand. "Cassandra, I cannot tell you what it means to see you here. I have never woken to a more beautiful sight in all my life. But there is something I must —"

He had no opportunity to say anything more. While he was trying to speak, Cassandra threw her arms around his neck and began to weep with relief. "You woke! You recognized me. Dear, dear Brandon!"

If he'd needed anything more to convince him of her true feelings, those warm, sweet tears would have been the final proof. Nothing she could say or do from now on would ever make him doubt again.

His past doubts had not been of *her*, he realized in that moment, but of himself and his ability to inspire the love of such a woman. Could whatever held her back from him have been rooted in that same poisonous soil of self-doubt? Reclined on the chaise with Cassandra kneeling on the floor beside him, Brandon wrapped his arms around her.

"Hush, my love, hush!" He pulled back her bonnet so he could nestle his cheek against her hair. "I promise you I am not dying. I am not even ill unless you count being heart-sick. In that case my condition was very grave indeed. But the sight of you has been just the tonic I needed. If we can come to an understanding as last, I believe I shall be cured altogether."

"Not ill?" Cassandra pulled back from him far enough to examine his countenance. She dashed the tears from her cheeks with the back of her hand. "I don't understand. Your cousin's letter said—"

"I can well imagine what it said." Brandon hoped she would not be too vexed when she learned the truth. "I shall have to lecture Imogene on the evils of deception, though it will not be easy when I am so pleased with the result."

"What have I done?" Cassandra tried to hide her face in her hands. "I burst in here like a raging lunatic!"

"No!" Brandon sat up then lifted Cassandra onto the chaise beside him. "You did what I would have done if I had received such a letter about you. In fact, I had every intention of calling at Noughtly Hall before I left Somerset. You may ask Imogene if you do not believe me. On second thought, perhaps my cousin is not the best witness in my defense."

He braced for a blast — perhaps accusations that he had put Imogene up to this cruel trick. Instead, Cassandra broke into wild laughter.

That had to be a good sign.

He must act swiftly, while her guard was down. "Whatever the reason for visiting your great-aunt, I swear it will not alter my feelings for you. If you are disgraced, time and marriage will remedy that. If you are with child, I will raise it and love it as my own."

His words turned Cassandra's laughter to astonishment. "You would do that for me? What if I bore a son?"

So that was her secret. During several long, dark nights, Brandon had confronted the possibility. He'd struggled with many aspects of such a situation, but in the end love had conquered all his reservations.

"If that is the case, the child would be my heir, as my brother is now. My father might not have approved, but I am done with allowing the mistakes of the past to poison my future … *our* future."

Since Cassandra seemed lost for words, Brandon rattled on. "Speaking of that, I have decided to contact my brother when I return to London. Hugh is no more responsible for the troubles in our family than I am. I hope we can be more like brothers in future, or at least friends."

Cassandra recovered her voice. "I believe such a connection will enrich your life immeasurably. Now, if you are willing to do so much for the sake of love, I must match your courageous example. The truth is, I am not with child nor have I been disgraced. Either would be impossible, since I have scarcely looked at another man since I first fell in love with you."

"You haven't … in all that time?" Suddenly Brandon knew how she must have felt when she discovered he was not ill — overwhelmed with relief but rather foolish as well.

Cassandra shook her head. "Never once. Though, in recent years it required no special effort. Suitors are not much interested in a lady my age unless she has a substantial fortune. I have scarcely a penny to my name."

She explained how her father had not survived long enough as Duke of Norland to provide for his daughters' futures. After everything she had told him about the man, Brandon doubted he would have made it a priority.

"I went to Noughtly Hall to act as a companion to my

great-aunt," Cassandra continued, "in exchange for my keep and a Season for Evie. That was the secret I could not bring myself to share with you. It seems ridiculous now to have kept it from you. But I hated to burden you with my penniless family. I could not bear to have you wed me out of pity then spend the rest of our marriage thinking I had wed you for your fortune."

Brandon thought back over the conversations they'd had while snowbound at the Martins' farm. "The things I told you about my parents' marriage must have made you believe it would be impossible for me to trust you."

Her sweet brow furrowed. "Would it not? If I had grown up in a family like yours, I am not certain I could trust myself, let alone anyone who would stand to gain so much by marrying me."

"Would you gain so much by marrying me?" Brandon gave a soft rueful chuckle. "Nothing that would signify without the priceless benefits you would bring. I cannot imagine a dowry more precious than your wit, your spirit and your kindness. In return, I must give you more than the things money can buy. If you will accept my proposal this time, I promise you my support, my trust and my love."

A soft, vulnerable mist rose in Cassandra's dark eyes. For an instant her indomitable chin quivered. "Am I worthy of such bounty? I know I told you and myself that I rejected your proposals to protect you. But now I know it was stubborn, selfish pride. That is one legacy I wish my father had never bequeathed to me. I cannot place the blame on him, though. I knew my fault, yet I did too little to correct it."

"Until today." Brandon caught her eye and gave a roguish wink. "When you thought I was ill you cast pride away and flew to my side. If I am not mistaken, you made rather a spectacle of yourself."

Cassandra pulled a wry face that lapsed into a self-conscious grin. "I did, didn't I? Well, I would do it again … especially if it was not all a trick of your cousin's."

Their eyes met and both began to sputter with laughter. The harder they tried to subdue it, the wilder it grew. Though Brandon wondered what his fellow guests might think, he gave himself up to it. In that burst of mirth, he sensed a purging of fear, mistrust, resentment and other dark emotions that had grown up like a wall of thorns between them.

When their frenzied laughter finally subsided, they each pulled out handkerchiefs and tenderly dried the other's tears.

Then Brandon slid off the chaise to kneel before Cassandra. "They say 'the third time is a charm' and I hope it will prove true in this case. For four years, I have loved you without hope and against my own inclination. Now I love you more than ever. If you will marry me, I am certain my love will only deepen with the years. Please say yes or I shall have to make a pest of myself by proposing to you on a regular basis."

"Surely you cannot doubt my answer." Cassandra slipped off the chaise to kneel with him — not a proud paragon on a pedestal, but a humble fellow supplicant. "It was assured from the moment I barged in here. I love you with all my heart. Though I hope to govern my pride in other respects, I shall always be proud to be your wife!"

Epilogue

Bath, June 1814

A S THE OPEN carriage drove toward Bath Abbey, Cassandra clasped the hand of her sister Viola, who was seated beside her. Across from them sat the viscountess, looking quite majestic in her full powdered wig, plumed hat and hooped silk gown.

Privately, Cassandra marveled at how close she and her redoubtable great-aunt had grown during the past several months. "Thank you again, Auntie, for hosting the wedding breakfast at Noughtly and inviting all the family to stay. It was a greater kindness than I deserve since I am deserting you to get married."

"Nonsense." The viscountess adjusted her parasol and dismissed Cassandra's thanks with an airy wave of her fan. "It is about time Noughtly had something to celebrate. Your marriage to Sir Brandon certainly qualifies. I approve of him greatly for making a love match."

"As do I." Cassandra winked at her sister, which made Viola chuckle.

Cassandra's affection and admiration for her sister had grown deeper than ever since her engagement to Brandon. Vi had been so transparently happy for her, so excited about every detail of the wedding and bridal tour. If she felt the slightest twinge of envy or regret over her own situation, she concealed it well. Cassandra was certain that even her rigorously truthful husband-to-be would not condemn her sister's behavior as deception, but rather approve it as thoughtfulness.

"Besides," the viscountess continued, "there is the family reputation to consider. It would not do for a daughter of the Whitney family to wed a wealthy baronet in some pokey little country church."

"I would happily wed my dearest Brandon anywhere," Cassandra declared. "Even over an anvil at Gretna Green."

Her ladyship shuddered. "Thank Heaven your bridegroom has more sense than that. Now is it agreed that Miranda will take your place as my companion? That is unless you will relent and allow me to have Evelina, instead."

Cassandra shook her head. "Brandon insists Evie must come to live with us. She and his cousin Imogene have become great friends."

In the past few months, Brandon's cousin had become a great deal more sensible and less apt to judge others based on their rank or fortune. Having been an only child, the young lady seemed delighted to find herself adopted into the Whitney's sisterly circle.

The carriage drew up in front of the Abbey where a liveried footman helped the ladies alight.

Once in they slipped inside the sanctuary through the elaborately carved Great West Doors; Viola paused to drape a veil of tulle and lace over Cassandra's bonnet.

Then she caught her sister in a warm embrace. "I wish you and Sir Brandon a lifetime of happiness, dearest Cassie!"

Cassandra clung to her sister. "I hope you and Miranda and Evie will be just as happy in love, one day! If it can happen to me, surely it can to all of you, since you are far more deserving."

"I do not believe that last part." For an instant, Viola's cheerful mask slipped. "As for the rest, it would be a fine thing indeed."

In her sister's gentle gaze, Cassandra glimpsed a trace of wistful doubt that such a future could be in store for her.

"Come girls." The viscountess beckoned them. "We must

not keep the guests and bridegroom waiting."

Viola took a deep breath and assumed a serene smile. Then she stepped forward and waited for the processional music to begin.

Meanwhile, Cassandra took her great-aunt's arm. "It is kind of you to walk me down the aisle. I know it is rather unorthodox, but considering I have so few male relatives …"

"I am a far more appropriate choice to give you in marriage than the new duke." The viscountess gave a sniff of derision. "He is practically a stranger and after the way he treated you and your sisters …"

The lady had no further opportunity to abuse His Grace, for the processional began and Viola started up the aisle.

As they proceeded toward the chancel at a stately pace, between the majestic columns of honey-gold stone, the viscountess murmured, "You might as well know, I mean to make you and your sisters my heirs. But you must not tell the others. I do not want them plagued with fortune hunters."

"Oh Auntie, how can I ever thank you?" Cassandra whispered, clutching her ladyship's arm tighter. Now Brandon would never have any reason to doubt that she had married him for love alone.

"Oh tush," replied the viscountess, her austere dignity softened by a smile.

In spite of the grand venue, this was a private wedding with a modest number of invited guests. They had been seated in the side-facing choir stalls that lined the chancel. As Cassandra passed the places usually reserved for the family of the groom, she spied Mr. and Mrs. Martin, beaming with pride of the best kind. She acknowledged them with a grateful smile. Without their help, would she be here now?

Then she turned her gaze toward the altar, where Brandon awaited her. Joy seemed to radiate from within him, illuminating his handsome features like the magnificent stained glass windows of the Abbey struck by the morning sun. The same sweet fire blazed in her heart — all the brighter for the four years of lonely darkness she had suffered without him.

The soaring music of the organ fell silent and the guests took their seats. The rector opened his prayer book and began to speak the familiar litany of the marriage service. Cassandra felt as if she were hearing every word for the first time.

"Who giveth this woman to be married to this man?" the rector asked.

"I do," the viscountess answered in a decisive tone that seemed to challenge anyone present to deny her right.

With a heart full of gratitude for second and even third chances, Cassandra took Brandon's hand and pledged herself to him *for better for worse, for richer for poorer*. The glow in his steadfast blue eyes assured her that he trusted she would love him just as much as if he had not a penny in the world.

A few moments later, Brandon slipped the wedding band onto her finger and endowed her with all his worldly goods. But it was the devotion of his faithful heart that would be her abiding treasure.

At last the ceremony concluded and the wedding party retired to the vestry to sign the parish register.

While Viola, Brandon's brother and the rector discretely looked the other way, Brandon claimed a swift tender kiss to seal their union.

When he surprised Cassandra by trying for another she blushed and whispered, "Is one not enough? Our guests are waiting."

"They can wait a little longer," Brandon flashed a grin of endearing impudence. "I have waited four years for this day and I reckon I deserve at least one kiss for every time I proposed to you."

Cassandra replied with a delighted chuckle. "If I had known that, I might have been tempted to refuse you a few more times."

"As long as you accepted in the end, my sweet!"

❄ ❄ ❄

Dear Reader,

Thank you for buying this book! I am very excited to release *Snowbound with the Baronet*, as it is the first novel I've written intentionally for independent publication.

I hope you enjoyed this story of Brandon and Cassandra's second chance at love. I have been a fan of this kind of romance ever since I read Jane Austen's *Persuasion*.

In case you're wondering (and I hope you are!) I plan to write more stories about Cassandra's sisters, Viola, Miranda and Evelina, their stepmother Letty and perhaps even Brandon's cousin Imogene. Though their father briefly held the title of duke, the Whitney sisters have not had an enviable life. Like the Dashwood sisters of *Sense and Sensibility*, the Bennett sisters of *Pride and Prejudice* and the Crawley sisters of *Downton Abbey*, they were short-changed by a social system that concentrated a family's wealth and property into the hands of the male heir.

Now that the duke is gone, his widow and daughters strive to make a new, happier life for themselves, sustained by their love for one another. If you would like to hear about the release of future books in the series, be sure to sign up for my newsletter, which includes exclusive excerpts and giveaways, information on special sales, first looks at cover art and news about future projects.

Happy Reading!
Deborah

Website: www.deborahhale.com
Facebook: www.facebook.com/AuthorDeborahHale
Goodreads: http://www.goodreads.com/
author/show/133710.Deborah_Hale
Pinterest: http://pinterest.com/hrwdebhale/

About the Author

Deborah Hale's first novel won the Golden Heart award for Long Historical and was nominated for a RITA award for Best First Book. Since then Deborah has written more than thirty books in the genres of historical romance, inspirational romance and otherworld fantasy. Her books have been translated into more than a dozen languages and sold millions of copies worldwide. Deborah invites you to visit her website for more information.

"Hale's characters are so finely created they become real in her readers' minds and hearts."
— syndicated romance reviewer, Sheryl Horst

Also Available

Confessions of a Courtesan

In a Stranger's Arms